CLEAN
WIN

CLEAN WIN

A Sam Quinton Mystery

KEVIN R. DOYLE

CAVEL PRESS

Kenmore, WA

CAMEL PRESS

A Camel Press book published by Epicenter Press

Epicenter Press
6524 NE 181st St.
Suite 2
Kenmore, WA 98028

For more information go to:
www.Camelpress.com
www.Coffeetownpress.com
www.Epicenterpress.com
www.kevindoylefiction.com

This is a work of fiction. Names, characters, places, brands, media, and incidents are either the product of the author's imagination or are used fictitiously.

Cover design by Scott Book
Design by Melissa Vail Coffman

Clean Win
Copyright © 2023 by Kevin R. Doyle

Library of Congress Control Number: 2022941083

ISBN: 978-1-68492-077-8 (Trade Paper)
ISBN: 978-1-68492-078-5 (eBook)

Printed in the United States of America

To Tyler B., Zane Z., and Parker H.,
former students who gave me the germ of the idea
that eventually became Sam Quinton.
Sorry, guys. No royalty split.

CHAPTER ONE

IF SOMEONE HAD EVER ASKED ME to make a list of the people I could never imagine gracing my gym with their presence, Lieutenant William Santiago of the Providence Police Department would have been up at the top. Yet there he was, on a bright Monday morning in early June, entering my establishment.

It was the lull period of the morning, too late for the up-and-coming white-collar types, doctors, lawyers, and assorted financial people, who rolled out of bed before five and headed down for a brisk workout before showing up at work to put in their sixteen-hour days, and too early for the small group of well-kept, upper class housewives of Providence who, their lives somehow firmly entrenched in the 1950's, came to break a sweat after seeing the hubby on his way to work and the kiddoes off to school.

Then again, here in early June in Missouri, school was out, and everyone knew the upper-class housewives would grudgingly resign themselves to spending the day with their kids. On the other hand, most of the offspring were such rotters that summer school was almost mandatory, and even for the others, it was an open secret the moms enrolled their kids anyway so they could continue to have their carefree mornings and afternoons.

At any rate, Santiago walked in and, trained investigator that he was, didn't take long to spot me among the five or six clients we had in the place. I was at the lat machine, struggling to get a few more reps out of what once upon a time wouldn't have seemed like all that much weight.

He headed my way, walking right past Lisa Nolan and Keri Eckland, my manager and her assistant, who huddled at the front counter going over membership application forms. The intensity of Santiago's movement made them look up, then over my way. I gave a quick shake of the head, and they went back to their work.

Santiago came up and stood there for a moment, looking down at me.

"Morning, Lieutenant," I said.

The cop nodded but didn't say anything. He had an odd look on his face, almost as if he were second guessing himself about something.

Santiago is somewhere in his mid-forties, probably a year or two younger than me, and stands five ten with thick black hair. Though not tall, there's a lean competence to his build that leads me to think few men would come out ahead in a tussle with him.

He was wearing a tan suit made, as far as I could tell, of silk with a silk maroon tie and light blue shirt. While I'm not enough of a clothes horse to tell the brand of his black loafers, they practically screamed Italian-made. His whole outfit probably cost as much, if not more, than my monthly mortgage payment on the gym.

Santiago dresses like this all the time, and he drives a late-model black Porsche Supra, the kind of car I couldn't even begin to squeeze into on my best days. Needless to say, there's a whole lot of speculation about how a police lieutenant can afford to live like he does.

"Something I can do for you?" I asked.

"I'd like to talk a few minutes if you don't mind, Quinton."

"Officially or unofficially?"

"Just want to talk," Santiago said.

I wiped off with a towel, stood up, and nodded towards the back end of the gym, down a short hall of which was my office.

As we headed that way, I caught Lisa Nolan's eye. She gave me a quizzical look, to which I shrugged and waggled my eyebrows.

When we got into my office, I sat down behind my desk but Santiago, despite the two empty chairs facing the desk, remained standing.

I wondered if he was worried about getting his suit soiled.

He looked around my office for a minute. "About what I'd expected," he said.

"Should I take that as a compliment?"

"If you want to."

The guy was starting to get on my nerves. I gestured towards the empty chairs and, after another long hesitation, he grimaced and sat down.

At least he didn't take out a hanky and wipe the seat off first.

"What can I do for you, Lieutenant?" I asked.

He glowered a moment before relaxing enough to sink back into the chair. "Laura Mosby," he said.

It took me a second or two of concentrating before I recognized the name. "Hair stylist," I said, "worked for one of the fancy shops here in town."

Santiago nodded.

"Was found strangled to death in her home a month or so back," I said.

"More like a little over two," the lieutenant said. "We found her at the tail end of March."

"From what I hear, the cops are stymied."

"We prefer to say we're pursuing all leads."

"I'll bet you do."

"Far as that goes," Santiago asked, "where'd you hear we're stuck? Sergeant Nichols been feeding you information on the sly?"

"Come on, Lieutenant. Why would he do that? And why would I care? I'm busy enough as it is without worrying about your business."

"You sure? From what I saw outside, you don't look all that busy."

"It's the middle of the morning," I said. "Drop in around early evening and the joint will be hopping."

"If you say so."

We sat there for another minute or two before I prodded the cop. "Laura Mosby."

"Right." Santiago sat a little straighter, as if pulling himself back on track. "We've got a possible suspect."

"From what the local news has reported, you've had more than one possible suspect."

Santiago nodded. "A former boyfriend, another even more former boyfriend, and a low-rent cousin who lives out of state."

"But?"

"But they were all dead ends. And now we've got someone new to look at."

"Which I'm guessing has something to do with why you're slumming enough to visit me this morning," I said. "So why not get to it. Who's the new favorite?"

Santiago looked away as he pressed his hands flat on his thighs. Despite our not-so-hot relationship, I decided to give him the time he needed.

He looked back my way, his expression as calm and controlled as I'd ever seen him.

"Bob Marlow," he said, so quietly I almost missed it.

I blinked a couple of times, processing the name.

"Bob Marlow," I repeated a few seconds later.

"Yeah," Santiago said, giving me half a nod.

"As in Mayor Bob Marlow?"

Only a quarter of a nod this time, if that. "Yeah."

"As in recently-announced candidate for governor Bob Marlow?"

No comment this time, except for Santiago giving me a dead-level stare.

"Well, shit," I said.

"Yeah," Santiago said.

CHAPTER TWO

"**I** NOTICE YOU'RE NOT RUSHING OUT to pick him up," I said a few minutes later.

Santiago nodded, that tight, controlled look still in his face. "Not yet."

"You going to?"

He didn't answer, at least not directly. "What do you know about our fearless leader?"

"I know it seems like he's been around for a while. I know on TV he comes across like the kind of guy who back in the day would wear Hair in a Can. I know if you transplanted him a couple of hundred miles south he'd fit right in as a small-town shitkicker. Other than that, not much."

"You know anything about his personal life or social activities?"

"Why the hell would I, Santiago? It's not exactly like the mayor and I travel in the same social circles. From what I've seen, he comes across as a good guy to have a beer or two with, though I've always had the sneaking suspicion he's damned lucky to have a good city manager."

Santiago nodded, as if I'd confirmed his beliefs. "The evidence we have isn't conclusive of murder."

An extra little level of tension had just crept into the room.

"What is it conclusive of?" I asked.

"Only that the Mosby girl and the mayor knew each other. Really well."

"Uh huh." I leaned back in my chair and laced my fingers behind my head. "What can I do for you, Lieutenant?"

He looked around the office for a second. "Can I speak confidentially?" he asked.

"I'd say the horse is already out of the barn on that one, but it depends."

"On what?"

"On whether you're thinking of hiring me or not."

"I can't do it with city funds," he pointed out.

"You could call me an independent consultant."

"And I'd have to fill out a three-page form explaining why your services were needed."

"Ouch," I said. "In that case, let's say this is an initial consultation."

"How much do you charge for initial consultations?"

"In most cases," I said, "no charge."

"Fair enough," Santiago said, "and I appreciate it."

"Why are your sights set on Marlow?"

"We finally got DNA back from the crime scene," Santiago said.

"Two months later? Didn't you expect a report by the next commercial break?"

Santiago grimaced. In the year or so I'd known the guy, he'd never acclimated to my sense of humor.

Or, far as I could tell, anyone else's.

"TV screws everyone up," he said. "Even on the supposedly realistic shows, the crime scene guys take off, and they're calling in with results before the cops finish their coffee break."

"But in the real world . . ."

"Takes months. Weeks if someone's really putting on the pressure."

"And for a single hair stylist in her twenties . . ." I said.

"Not all that much pressure," Santiago said.

"As I recall, the young woman was found dead in her bedroom."

"Right. Fully stripped and raped before she was done in."

"I hate to be beyond grisly," I said, "but are you sure she was raped before she was dead?"

Santiago grimaced even harder. The tough former Chicago

cop was really having trouble with this one. "Near as the ME can determine."

"Can he tell for sure it was actually rape?"

Santiago lifted his hands palms upwards. "Looks like it. The place was a shambles, her clothes thrown all around the room, and there was the appropriate bruising. Looks right."

"But not conclusive," I said. "It could have just been rough play."

"Could have been, though judging by the way she ended up, I doubt it."

I was willing to take his cop's instincts on that one. "What kind of hit on Marlow?"

"Semen."

My gut roiled a bit at the next question. "In her or somewhere else?"

"Both. In her and a little bit smeared on the sheets."

The light dawned, and I could see exactly what was driving Santiago nuts. "Proof the good mayor was in the bedroom with her but not that he killed her."

The cop cracked a slight grin as he lifted his hand in my direction, formed a pistol and shot me with his forefinger. "I was in the office last Saturday, only time I could catch up on paperwork. Jorgenson, the head honcho at the state lab, called me directly."

"Rather than going to the detectives working the case?" I asked.

Santiago nodded. "Turns out they went the extra mile, once they had a type, and went looking for matches. Jorgenson has a daughter about the same age as the Mosby girl. Although he wasn't really expecting a hit, he got one."

"How?" I asked. "When would the mayor have ever had his DNA typed?"

"Turns out, though you wouldn't know it to look at him, he's registered as a captain in the National Guard. For quite a while now, all military members have their DNA on file."

"In case they get killed defending us from the godless commies?" I asked.

"More like if they come up dead or missing during national disasters. Took forever and a day before it finally pinged."

"Any other samples or matches?" I asked.

Santiago grinned, though in a rather sickly way. "You're pretty good at this investigation stuff, aren't you Quinton?"

"I had a good teacher," I said.

"After the initial heads-up, Jorgenson sent the entire report to me directly. There were a few stray hairs and such here and there. Nothing else that snagged a match."

"Then the only definite match to someone in the room shortly around the time of death is the mayor," I said.

"Uh huh."

"Geez, Lieutenant, what a mess."

"Got that right."

"All right, let me make sure I've got this. You have evidence of the mayor's presence in her house, more specifically her bedroom, but no evidence of him as the killer."

"Uh huh."

"Based on what you have so far, standard procedure would call for you to haul the guy in and interrogate him."

"That's right," Santiago said.

"But if you did have evidence of him as the killer, it would be a lot easier to haul him in for questioning. No way anyone could fault you then."

"Correct."

"And if you yank him in and it turns out he's not the killer, that he was just having a little fun on the side—"

"You see my problem."

I shook my head a couple of times, trying to get my thinking clear. "Who all knows about the DNA report?"

"At the moment, just me and Jorgenson."

I stared at the big cop for a moment, my breath not coming easily. "You haven't even told the detectives investigating the case?"

A bit of a glare came into Santiago's eyes. "That's exactly right. If they saw the report, they'd go off to do the right thing and haul the mayor in."

"Then again, if he's innocent . . ."

"Then he calls out the dogs, and a lot of good people's careers crash to the ground."

"Josh?" I asked.

Santiago took a deep breath and eased it out. "I haven't yet informed Sgt. Nichols either. I plan to tell him before long, but I want it to be at a time of my choosing."

"Christ, you really are going out on a limb, aren't you?" I asked.

"Believe it."

"Who are the primaries on the case?"

"Reynolds and Krenshaw."

I stood up and walked over to a mini fridge I keep in the corner. I picked up the coffeepot sitting on top and glanced at Santiago. He shook his head. I poured a cup for myself and brought it back to my desk.

"How long you think you've got?" I asked.

"You mean before the detectives start to wonder where their report is?"

I nodded.

"I figure a couple of days, four at the most, is all I can hold them off."

"And in that time you want me to find—"

"Some other proof, something tangible can back us up."

"In order to arrest the mayor?"

"Or to clear him. Either way, I—what is it, Quinton?"

I paused a moment, choosing my words more carefully than I had in a long time. "Cards on the table, Lieutenant."

"Okay."

"There's been a lot of speculation about you since you arrived in town."

"Uh huh."

"Mainly about," I gestured towards him, "how you manage to live so well on a lieutenant's salary."

"Meaning you're wondering if I'm corrupt in some way."

"Well," I said, "yeah."

"My personal affairs are nobody's business, Quinton. But I'll tell you this. At the moment, all I'm interested in is bringing that girl's killer to justice, whether the mayor or someone else."

"And it would sure help if you could definitively check the box on him one way or the other before moving forward."

"Which is what I need you for. This is too dicey to bring the full department into it right now."

"I get it," I said. "You want a clean win."

"A what?"

I jerked my thumb behind me towards the Midwest Wrestling League championship belt hanging on the wall. "In my former profession, when you won a match without any friends helping, or using any dirty tricks, when it was clear and straightforward you were on the right side, it was called a clean win."

"Except that, in your former profession, everyone knew who was going to win ahead of time, right? Even the refs?"

I grinned at the cop. "Especially the refs. Who do you think controlled what went on during the match?"

Santiago nodded. "That's the idea then, Quinton. I need a referee, to protect my people and the department."

"There's one other thing you should consider," I said.

"Which is?"

"I'm not sure you can keep this quiet as long as you think. This is a juicy little bit of gossip. How long you think before someone at the lab spills it to the press?"

Santiago's face reddened a bit. "Thanks, Quinton. I've been doing my best not to think about that."

"Still has to be thought about. I'm not sure I can do a thorough enough job in only a few days, maybe less."

The cop tensed up, his shoulders causing the light silk of his suit to ripple. "All it will be is a rumor. Unverifiable. And any of those people know it will be their job if they say anything."

"Uh huh."

"Uh huh," Santiago mimicked. "Even if it goes down like that, it will be something out of my hands."

"Could round up everyone involved and put them in the basement of the city building until it all gets sorted out."

"Believe it or not, if I was back in Chi I could probably do just that. Not so much in a small town like this."

I prefer to think of Providence as either a big town or a small city, but it didn't seem the time to quibble the point.

"What about payment?" I asked. "After all, I do this kind of thing for a living."

Santiago frowned for a second. "How about this? At the moment, I can't have any record of paying you to interfere in police work. What say I pay you under the table, and if things turn out okay, I can go ahead and put in a voucher and backdate it."

"And if things don't turn out right?" I asked.

Santiago shrugged. "Then I'll be out of a job, and you'll have to do what you can to get your money from the next guy."

I considered that for a moment. "Can you afford my rates?"

"Depends on what they are."

I quoted him my standard daily rate, and the lieutenant shook his head.

"People actually pay you that much?"

"From time to time," I said. "Quality ain't cheap."

"Neither is desperation. Okay, Quinton, you got a deal. What do we do next?"

I reached into my desk and pulled out a small spiral bound notebook and pen.

Okay, I'm old-fashioned. Sue me.

"Next," I said, "is you fill me in on everything about the case. I'm assuming the less electronic records, the better?"

"You assume right."

I clicked the pen into action. "Then start talking, Lieutenant."

CHAPTER THREE

SANTIAGO SPENT ANOTHER HALF HOUR IN my office, walking me through the investigation, both the moves taken by the primary detectives, Matt Reynolds and Abbie Krenshaw, and all sorts of ancillary activities. As was usually the case, my buddy Det. Sergeant Josh Nichols was technically supervising the investigation, with Lieutenant Santiago looking on from above.

All of which changed, of course, when the DNA report on the evidence gathered at the crime scene arrived. As Santiago had told me, once Jorgenson at the lab had seen the hit, he'd called the lieutenant straight up.

I could only imagine what Santiago had felt when he'd processed what Jorgenson had told him.

"You realize," I said at one point, "as you're telling me all this that a few minutes ago you were ready to tear into Nichols at the idea he was feeding department info to me."

"Nichols is a sergeant. I'm a lieutenant."

"Aw," I said, "that clears it up. Aren't Reynolds and Krenshaw going to be pissed at you for withholding the information from them? It is their case after all."

"If they are, they'll get over it," the lieutenant replied. "Technically, I'm not withholding anything. I'm simply keeping it on my desk until one or the other asks for it."

While I wasn't all that sure the detectives in question would see it his way, departmental politics wasn't my worry. I kept quiet and continued taking notes as Santiago continued spooling out info. It took him some time to run dry.

"The best way to do this," I said, "would be to begin at the beginning and basically redo the entire investigation over again."

"Why?" Santiago asked. He no doubt knew the answer as well as I did but wanted to reassure himself as to my thinking.

"Because going straight at the mayor would be too risky," I said. "If I start investigating him directly, it won't be all that long before he finds out. And he'll wonder who set an independent operator like me on to him."

"Which could lead right back to the force," Santiago said.

I nodded. "It's going to happen before long anyway. In a city this small, it'll be hard to keep my movements quiet."

Santiago shook his head. "My people have already gone over the preliminary steps. What would be the point of . . ."

"You guys did a standard investigation," I said, "but when you started, you didn't have an obvious suspect in mind, other than possibly the ex-boyfriend."

"So you're going to investigate from scratch already knowing who you're looking to implicate?"

"That's the idea, Lieutenant. And I'm guessing you'll want me to do this out of sight of your primaries."

"As much as possible. Reynolds and Krenshaw are good cops, and they don't deserve to be shut out of their own investigation."

"Which you happen to be doing," I pointed out.

The tough cop grimaced. "Only temporarily. It's for their own good. If you can at least get me weighing more heavily one way or the other, I'll be able to protect them."

I wasn't all that convinced that protecting his subordinates was the top thing on Santiago's mind. If I'd had to guess, I saw it just as likely he was looking out for himself first and his detectives second. If they saw the lab report and plowed ahead, no matter right or wrong, Santiago would be seen as the one in charge, and the greatest heat would come down on him.

As I said, though, department politics wasn't my thing. The lieutenant and I settled on three days' pay to begin with, which he managed to pull out of his wallet and hand over. Almost made me wish I'd quoted a higher rate.

CHAPTER FOUR

After Santiago left, I finished up a few things and headed out. I stopped by the front counter to let Lisa Nolan know I was going to be more out than in for a few days. Lisa, more than capable of running the gym by herself, merely nodded as I headed out the door.

Not for the first time, I worried the next time I showed up I'd find the locks changed and her in full ownership of the place.

She's that good at her job.

I first met Lisa when she showed up and began working out some years back. She's mid-twenties, about five two with bright red hair and green eyes. A health nut her whole life, when she first started coming around my place, she was the co-owner, with her boyfriend at the time, of a vegetarian café. They lived and worked together, and let's just say the boyfriend wasn't the nicest guy around. More than once, I saw her working out with faint bruises on her arms or slight blackening under her eyes.

After a while, I couldn't take it anymore and had a talk with her. That led to a longer, slightly more forceful talk with the boyfriend, which resulted in them splitting up and selling off the business.

While Lisa was now out of a rotten relationship, the downside was she was now out of work and had no place to live. After we hashed it out for a while, we decided she would come to work for me. The kicker to the whole deal was a small room I have on the second story, which she used for a while as an apartment.

All that was years ago, and now she more or less runs the place, and has since moved into an actual apartment. All in all, one of the smartest hires I ever made.

Leaving the gym, I climbed into my cashmere pearl Cherokee and headed home, as I drove reviewing the basics of the case as Santiago had laid them out to me. Most of it was familiar from following the local news for the last few months, though some of it was stuff the cops were holding close to the vest.

LAURA MOSBY WAS TWENTY-NINE YEARS OLD at the time of her death. She'd been a hair stylist for nearly five years, and for the last three had worked at a place down on the south side of town called *Extensions*. I thought the name was kind of hokey, but I call my gym The Blaster, so what do I know?

Extensions was the kind of place a guy like myself had heard of but never set foot in. Had I done so, they would have taken one look at my mop, reaching almost to my shoulders, thinning a bit in front and with almost as much gray as the blond color that had given me my wrestling name of The Blond Bomber, and turned me right around and out again.

According to her friends and co-workers, Laura had recently broken up with her latest boyfriend and as far as they knew hadn't yet become serious about dating anyone else. She left the salon one Thursday night shortly after closing, not scheduled to return to work until the following Tuesday.

That Saturday her mother, who lives in Akron, Ohio, got a bit concerned when Laura didn't make her customary once-a-week call but didn't think much about it until most of Sunday had gone by with still no word from her daughter. She spent Monday afternoon calling the few friends of her daughter that she knew, but none of them had seen her in several days either.

However, one of them did mention she and Laura had had a date to go shopping the day before, and when Laura didn't show up or answer her phone or texts, the friend had swung by her house, only to find it darkened and with no answer to her knocks.

Between the two of them, they got concerned enough to call

the cops and ask for a welfare check, and approximately 7:30 that evening a patrol car had swung by and, using the friend's knowledge of where Laura kept her spare key, the officers had opened the door and come upon a crime scene.

Nothing in the living room or kitchen of the small house looked disturbed although the officers' noses clearly indicated to them something was up.

They found the young victim in her bedroom, nude and crumpled up on her bed. Even a quick eyeball inspection revealed the telltale marks of some sort of strangling, with the ME finally determining someone had choked her to death, more than likely with bare hands.

As Santiago had said, a cursory forensics examination revealed the young woman had had sex at some point before her death, whether consensual or not remained undetermined.

The cops went through the usual motions, beginning with picking up and interrogating Ryan Granger, Laura's former boyfriend, but when it turned out he had a rock solid alibi, and they could come up with no witnesses claiming the young man harbored a grudge of any sort against Laura, they'd let him go.

A few checks on the other men in her life they knew about had also come up empty, and for the last two months the detectives had first run around in circles, then gradually put the case on the back burner.

Until last Saturday, when Santiago had been in his office catching up on paperwork and received the call that turned the entire case upside down.

I ENTERED MY APARTMENT AND CHANGED INTO SLACKS, a clean tee-shirt and silk blazer, clothing probably slightly more acceptable to the clientele of a place like *Extensions*, then climbed back in the car and headed out again. By now, we were coming up on late morning traffic, though this early into summer it wasn't too bad. During the school year, when our three colleges are in full session, daytime traffic in Providence can really test one's patience.

I parked the Cherokee, checked one more time in the rearview mirror to make sure I didn't look too scruffy, then climbed out and headed into the salon. There were, at quick glance, about twenty stations with around half of them occupied. The various stylists all looked to be in their late twenties to early thirties, and at a glance I didn't see a one that didn't sport some sort of visible tattoo or piercing.

A pert little blonde stood behind the front podium, made of oak and barely standing up under the weight of half a dozen exotic, potted plants. She had two of the largest dimples I've ever seen.

"Is the manager in?" I asked.

"Concerning?"

I pulled out my wallet and showed the photostat of my investigator's license.

The young woman looked at it, then back up at me. "For real?"

I gave her a smile. It was my "most innocent in the world" smile. I'd perfected it back in my wrestling days. It used to come in handy whenever I'd pulled some dirty trick on my opponent behind the referee's back and wanted to convince the ref of my angelic intentions.

"For real," I said.

"What's this about?" Her eyes were snapping. Obviously, talking to a real live PI was the high point of her workday.

Maybe the week.

"It's about something I need to discuss with the manager. Sorry."

"She's kind of busy. First day of the week, you know."

"I'm sure, but look at it this way. You'd be dragging her away from the drudgery of inventorying the bottles of coloring fluid, or whatever it is she's doing back there."

The blonde giggled as she picked up the phone resting on her podium. "That's not what she's doing, but it's almost as boring." I turned my back and walked a few steps away out of politeness, as she spent a minute or so chatting with someone named Kylie before hanging up.

"She'll be up here in a sec."

It was closer to ten seconds before a tall black woman with copper-colored hair came striding from the back part of the salon. She was wearing a solid black, strapless dress that ended just above her

knees, fit her like a sheath, and demonstrated the lady knew how
to keep herself in shape.

She looked familiar, though offhand I couldn't place her.

"Kylie Rogers," the woman said as she came alongside of me.
"Can I help you, Mr. Quinton?"

I took her hand, a bit surprised she knew me. I hadn't heard the
podium girl give my name.

"I'm almost a regular at your gym," she said with a smile, "at
least, as regular as my six-day work week allows me to be."

"Good to know," I said. "Is there some place we can talk
privately?"

She motioned, and I followed her the length of the salon to her
office in the back.

It was a cluttered little place, not much more than a broom
closet, which indicated the upkeep on the sumptuous front part
cost every penny it looked. Between unopened cases of hair
product stacked on the floor, three large green filing cabinets,
and a row of steel shelves that took up one wall and contained
more shipping cases, the place barely held room for the one chair
I could sit down in.

"What can I do for you?" Kylie Rogers asked, perching herself
on two stacked boxes of conditioner. "I'm guessing this has something to do with Laura?"

I stared at her a minute. "Why would you say that?"

She shrugged. "Nothing else has gone on around here I can
think of that would bring out a detective. Who are you working
for? Her mother?"

"Sorry, Miss Rogers—"

"Please, you've seen me in your place when I've been soaking in
sweat and out of breath. Call my Kylie."

"Okay, Kylie. Sorry but I can't really say who my client is."

"I understand, even if it's obviously her."

If she wanted to think Laura Mosby's mother, no doubt despair-
ing after months with no movement on her daughter's case, had
hired an investigator, all the better. Way I saw it, although digging
up evidence that would either implicate or clear the mayor was my

primary job, keeping Santiago's hiring of me confidential came in a close second.

"So what can I do for you?" Kylie asked.

"Well, I've got several questions about Laura. Her clients, what she told you or any of her co-workers about her personal life, if she ever mentioned anyone she was having trouble with. Things like that."

"Sounds like a lot of talking," she said with a grin.

"If you don't have the time now, I understand. Maybe we can make an appointment."

"Screw the appointment. You're giving me a choice between helping to find a killer and working on last month's bills all day? Hell, the bills can wait."

"Glad to hear it," I said. "Was Laura seeing anyone special?"

Kylie Rogers frowned a bit, not so much at me as in concentration. "Wow, you don't waste time, do you?"

"Not if I can help it. Was she?"

"She had a boyfriend for quite a while, but they broke up about a month before she died."

"That would be Ryan Granger?" I asked.

"It would."

"You know why they broke up?"

Kylie pursed her lips for a moment as she thought. "Not really. Laura would mention it every now and then, but never got all that specific."

"Have any ideas at all?" I asked.

She shook her head. "Sorry."

"Is there anyone else I could talk to who could give me more detail?" I asked.

"You mean like one of the other stylists?"

"That would be the first direction."

"Could be, but doubtful. The only time they're together is out on the floor, and with customers around, no one talks much about personal stuff. At least, nothing that personal."

"She associate with any of the others outside of work?"

"Not really. You work long hours, and when the shift is over, usually the last thing anyone wants to do is hang out with someone they've just spent the last nine or ten hours standing next to."

"You guys ever take lunch together? Coffee breaks? Anything like that?"

Kylie shrugged. "Sure. But Laura was always a little standoffish even then. A little like she was too good to hang out with the other girls."

I wasn't entirely willing to take Kylie's word for it. Even though she sounded truthful enough, I could think of a handful of reasons why she'd want to deflect attention from her workers. Besides, one of the first things Santiago and his crew would have done was extensively interview all of her employees, and I doubted I could uncover anything they hadn't. If I needed to look for more info, I'd just call up the lieutenant.

"You have any idea if it was Laura or Ryan who did the actual breaking up?"

Kylie shook her head. "Like I said, I never could get a clear read on that. For all I know, it could have been a mutual thing. She never said enough to know either way."

"Would it be sexist for me to point out that young females looking for sympathy tend to tell each other intimate details about guys?"

Kylie laughed. "It would be entirely sexist, Mr. Quinton. And it would also be entirely true. But I think you need to look for friends elsewhere. She just wasn't all that close to anyone here."

"Any other guys she mentioned or that you noticed hanging around?" I asked.

"Sure. But none who set off my creep vibes."

"She have any male clients?"

Kylie hesitated, as if she could guess where I was heading. "Some. All of us have clients of both genders, plus a few beyond the standard two. Most of the time, though, it's women."

"Any Laura was concerned about?" I didn't want to come right out and mention the mayor's name, and I wasn't all that sure Kylie, even as helpful as she appeared, would squeal on such a powerful client.

If in fact he was one. In his two decades in Providence politics, Bob Marlow had been accused of a lot of things, but rarely being a dummy. Visibly flirting with or picking up the woman who cuts his hair, right in front of God and everyone, didn't seem like the sort of move he would play.

"Not that she mentioned to me," Kylie said. "And I can tell you right now that if she'd said anything to any of the other girls, the cops would have drug it out of them. When they came around to question us, it was damned near an interrogation."

Pretty much as I'd already figured. Once more, if I wanted to know more along those lines, Santiago would surely have the info.

We talked for a few more minutes, but Kylie either didn't know or wouldn't divulge anything else. She claimed to have no idea, beyond the salary she earned, about Laura Mosby's financial situation. She also said she didn't really know who any of Laura's friends outside of work were. She'd heard some names mentioned now and then, only first names and not many details beyond that.

As far as I could determine, or that she let on, Laura Mosby's boss had no idea the mayor had any connection with the dead girl at all. And since the mayor's link to the case, if any, was what Santiago needed me to check out, eventually I thanked her, said I'd mention to Lisa Nolan to give her a week's use of the gym free of charge for taking the time to talk to me, and headed out.

CHAPTER FIVE

A FTER LEAVING *EXTENSIONS*, I TOOK THE OBVIOUS next step and set out to talk to Ryan Granger, the most recent former boyfriend. While the cops had cleared Laura's ex, their interrogation and investigation of him would have followed the usual pattern for such cases. Naturally, Santiago's detectives wouldn't have been looking for anything that would tie Laura to Mayor Marlow, giving me actually two advantages going in.

I was looking for something that would connect Laura to said mayor, and I didn't have to worry about trying to prove the kid guilty.

About three o'clock that afternoon, I pulled up outside of his work place, a local distribution center for a major retailer. The parking lot was nearly full, and as I looked the place over, I noticed a larger than expected number of fairly expensive and well-cared for cars and trucks. There may have been a clunker or two somewhere in the lot, though I couldn't see any, and most of the vehicles looked, at most, no more than two or three years old.

I began revising my life-long prejudices about the value of manual labor.

Stepping inside the building, air-conditioned to somewhere in the low seventies, I stopped to look around. The place had a small, glass-enclosed lobby up front, and through the rear wall I could see the rear section with probably a dozen loading bays, three of them empty at this time of day, and the others occupied by trucks being unloaded by forklifts.

As I stood there watching for a moment, it didn't look as if any of the workers were over thirty.

Down the hall from the lobby lay what I assumed was a series of offices, and the heavy iron door that let out into the loading area had an "Employees Only" sign about chest high.

From one of the office doors, a young blond man stepped out, clipboard in hand, and began heading my way. He looked a little puzzled when he saw me. I put the most natural grin possible on my face and walked up to him.

"Excuse me," I said as I stepped in front of him, "Ryan Granger?"

The youngster glanced out at the loading area, looking in both directions. "I don't see him out there, so he's probably on his break right now. Lounge is down that hall and on the left."

He pointed me in the direction he'd come from and, nodding my thanks, I headed off.

It was a typical working facility break room: a dozen white plastic tables scattered around, a handful of black plastic chairs positioned every which way, and a bank of vending machines against one wall. I saw three men and one woman taking their downtime at the moment, each sitting at a separate table with some sort of beverage and their phones arrayed in front of them.

Going by the description Santiago had given me, only one could have been Granger.

I walked over to him, a tall, thin guy with longish blond hair, a cup of coffee on the table in front of him and his phone in his hands. He was so focused on whatever pranced across his phone he didn't even notice my approach until I was a foot away.

Even though from a distance he looked like a fairly athletic young man, up close I could see the telltale loosening of the jowls and puffiness around the eyes that indicated he was sliding out of shape.

"Ryan Granger," I said as he looked up.

He didn't answer at first, instead giving me a long, careful look over.

He obviously didn't like what he saw.

"Not interested," he said before turning back to look down at his phone.

I sighed, as loudly and dramatically as possible, and sat down, not across from him but at his elbow.

Granger turned to look at me again.

"Whoever you are, just get lost. Okay?" he said.

"Make me," I said.

"Huh?" Now the kid looked a little confused.

"I said if you want me to get lost, make me. Or we can sit here and talk for a few minutes like decent people, and I'll go on my way."

"Talk about what? Who the hell are you anyway, old man?"

Shaking my head at the "old man" comment, I pulled out the photostat of my license, showed it to him. His shoulders slumped, and he became even more downcast than before.

"Let me guess. Laura's family asked you to check me out, right?"

"Why do you say that?"

"Because I've been getting hate calls from them for the last two months. One of her brothers even came all the way here from Akron to follow me around for a while. Hiring a dude like you seems the next logical step."

"They know the cops cleared you?" I asked.

Granger nodded. "Of course. The cops even went to the trouble of calling the family up and talking to them about it directly. Hell, I even asked that guy detective, what's his name?"

"Reynolds," I said.

"Yeah, him. I even called him up one day and asked him to talk to her mom again, make it clear that I was off the hook. A few days later, he called me back and said he'd passed on the word."

"They leave you alone after that?"

"Obviously not. After all, you're here doing their dirty work for them."

I shook my head. Granger gave me a long, searching look without saying anything.

He also didn't seem very bothered. As I sat there, he went back to staring at the phone.

"I'd like to ask you some questions," I said in as polite a tone as I could muster.

"Fuck off," Granger said, still not looking up.

"'Scuse me?"

The kid put his phone down, picked up his cup and took a swig of coffee, then set the cup back on the table.

"I said fuck off," he said, finally meeting my gaze. "You're not a cop, so I don't have to tell you nothing. And while I'm sorry she's dead, Laura's mom can kiss my ass. I didn't have anything to do with it, in fact hadn't seen her for weeks before it happened, and I'm tired of their constant hassling me."

"That's your final word?" I asked.

"That's it. Now if you don't mind, old man, I've got about five minutes left on my break before I have to get back to work. And I'd sure like a whole hell of a lot to sit here quietly for that five minutes. Got me?"

The kid was either a lot tougher or a lot more stupid than he looked. Either way, I could kind of see his point. According to Santiago, he'd been cleared every which way and was so far off the suspect list he probably couldn't see it.

I'd be bothered too if I was him.

I wasn't done with Granger, but I figured there wasn't any need to let him know at the moment. Not here at his work, where no doubt he had all sorts of friends to call on if things got out of hand.

"Sorry to bother you," I said as I got up and walked away.

I'd made it halfway out of the breakroom when Granger called out to me.

"Hey, PI."

I stopped and turned his way. "Yeah?"

"Don't come around here bothering me again, and don't go snooping around my friends or anything. I had nothing to do with Laura's murder, and that's how it's going to stay. I don't care what the Mosby's think."

I nodded, as if totally cowed by his bluster, and headed on out.

CHAPTER SIX

Pulling out of the parking lot at Granger's workplace, I drove a whopping two blocks before turning the Cherokee around and easing up to a convenient curb. I then made a phone call to a friend of mine, who works in a certain state office, and asked her to get some information for me.

About twenty minutes later she called back and provided the model, color, and tag number of Granger's car. I tapped the info into my phone, thanked her for her little bit of skullduggery, and promised her, of course, I'd get tickets for her and her husband for the next KC Royals home game.

I'd barely hung up when my phone buzzed again. Glancing at the display, I gulped with a bit of nervousness.

"'Yello," I said.

"What are you up to, Blondie?"

Detective Sergeant Josh Nichols is one of the few people who can call me by my old wrestling name without getting a glower in return.

"Not doing much, what's up with you?" I said.

There was a slight pause before Nichols replied. "Have you spoken to Santiago lately?"

"Your boss?" I said. "Why do you think he'd want to talk to me?"

"He was asking about you the other day. Asked me what you'd been up to recently."

"Maybe he's become a new fan and wants my autograph," I said.

"Don't think so, seeing as he was frowning while he asked."

If Nichols and I had been face-to-face, I would have shrugged and done my best to look clueless, which some people say isn't all that hard for me. Since we weren't face-to-face, I had to put as much disinterest into my tone as I could.

"Don't know what to tell you, Josh. Maybe he's mad about something and is getting ready to make a run at me."

"That would be more likely," Nichols said. "He doesn't seem to have much use for private operators, or for his own people, far as that goes. You working on anything at the moment?"

"Nothing I could imagine your boss getting upset about." Which, if you think about it, was the absolute truth.

"Okay, whichever, may want to watch your back for a while, make sure you're not treading on any toes you shouldn't be."

"Will do," I said as I rung off.

Settling back in my seat more, I dialed up a 1980's music channel and leaned back to wait.

After fifteen minutes or so of mindless sitting and listening, I got antsy and placed another call.

Dr. Talia Sanderson answered on the second ring. "Hello?"

"Guess who," I said.

The lady didn't answer, and I had the feeling that had I been standing in front of her, her scornful look would have withered me down to nothing.

"You're not calling to cancel tonight, are you?" she finally asked.

"Why would you think that?"

"Because you're not exactly known for calling up to pass the time of day," she said.

"Maybe I wanted to save you, spring you out of one of those long, boring academic meetings that take up all your time."

"Maybe, but I doubt it. What's up?"

"I may have to cancel tonight," I said.

"Gee, I never would have guessed. Good thing I got to choose the restaurant. If you don't show up, I'll just order double and scarf it all down myself."

"Are university deans allowed to say words like scarf?" I asked.

"They are if they're socializing with guys like you. You really bailing out?"

"Okay, so cancel was probably too strong a word. How about delay for a few hours?"

"You on a case?" A new level of seriousness had entered her tone.

Talia Sanderson was the dean of social sciences at the largest of our three local universities. I'd met her a few months back while investigating a murder case that managed to entangle two of her professors.

"Yeah," I said, "nothing dangerous."

"How not dangerous?"

"Right about now I'm waiting to accost a minor witness, a kid in his twenties who I'm pretty sure has absolutely no connection to the crime."

"Accost?" Talia said.

"I've been studying the dictionary at nights, hoping to impress you."

"You'd impress me a lot more by showing up safe and sound on my doorstep. And does your license permit accosting?"

I moved my phone away a bit so she wouldn't hear me clear my suddenly-tight throat. Talia and I had only gone out a handful of times. Neither of us seemed to be looking for anything deep and meaningful at the moment, but we'd discovered we enjoyed each other's company quite a bit.

"How about I say I'm waiting to mildly annoy him. And I may not be late at all," I said. "This guy shouldn't take too long."

"In that case, I'll keep your seat at the restaurant warm."

"Sounds like a plan," I said.

"The case anything you can talk about?"

I thought for a moment about Lt. Santiago, and the position the new information about the Laura Mosby case had put him in. "Not really, much as I'd love to. Let's just say it's major and leave it at that."

A moment of silence stretched over the miles between us. "Serious like the Felix Thayer deal?"

Thayer had been the professor whose problems had first caused Talia and me to cross paths.

"Something along those lines," I said.

Another long pause, even more dramatic than the first. "Come by whenever you can," she said, "and take care of yourself."

We disconnected, and I settled in to continue waiting.

CHAPTER SEVEN

TURNED OUT, WASN'T THAT LONG. About half an hour later, the chain link gates which sealed off the center's employee parking lot opened up and a line of vehicles started exiting, about a third turning to the east and the rest heading west. I kept my eyes peeled for a blue 86 Corvette, and tagged it as the fifth car out.

It occurred to me Granger had a fairly cushy job if he was allowed to take coffee breaks within an hour of getting off for the day.

Fortunately for me, the 'Vette turned east, away from the majority of the traffic, which would make it easier to keep it in my sights.

Unfortunately for me, I was parked heading west, so I had to do some fancy jockeying against the oncoming traffic in order to get myself situated to where I could follow Granger.

It was an easy tail, primarily because I assumed my quarry wasn't expecting anyone to be following him.

Of course, I had his address, information provided by the same kind soul who'd given me his car make and tag. Even without her help, I could have easily located his residence on my own. I followed him anyway because I wanted to see where he went and what he did.

I considered it a good chance a young guy like him would potentially have several stops to make before calling it a night, and I figured it wouldn't hurt to learn as much about his doings as possible before taking another run at him, in a situation where it would be more one-on-one.

Turned out I was beyond overthinking things, as Granger headed straight home, in his case a somewhat secluded condo on the far west side of town. He pulled into the overhang driveway of a blue, two-story unit with a balcony with a wire mesh screen separating it from the elements.

I'm no real estate agent, but at a glance I'd guess the place, especially considering current prices, probably went for somewhere north of two hundred thou.

Pretty nice pickings for a guy who worked at a warehouse.

By now, I was really revising those previous opinions of the benefits of manual labor.

I tooled my Cherokee a couple of blocks past before pulling it into the curb. On the off-chance things went south, I didn't want some random witness to remember my vehicle parked outside of Granger's place.

Plus, I figured it wouldn't hurt to keep him from getting a good look at my ride.

Under ordinary circumstances, I wouldn't have worried much. I didn't have any real mischief in mind, and if I got into a sticky situation, I had a fairly good in with the cops in town, and things could be ironed out without much sweat.

And if things for some reason got super tense, my good buddy Det. Sgt. Josh Nichols could do the bailing out.

Under ordinary circumstances.

At the moment, though, things weren't all that ordinary. I had to do my best to stay as much on the down low as possible because of the need to shelter Lt. Santiago from any blowback, at least until he was ready to go on the record for or against Mayor Marlow.

Still, I needed to talk to the former boyfriend, and while he hadn't been all that forthcoming at work, here at his house I figured I could reason with him a little better.

It only took me a few minutes to make it from where I'd parked to his house, and I gave it another five minutes for him to get somewhat settled in before knocking on the door.

I had to knock a second time before I heard footsteps coming and the door flew open. Granger stood in the doorway, clad only in gym shorts and tennis shoes.

"What the hell?" he said. "What are you doing here?"

In shorts and with his shirt off, I figured he'd been about to work out when I'd interrupted. "Got a few more questions for you, Ryan. Now a good time?"

Unclothed as he was, I could see even more clearly the evidence his body was starting to go soft. Even so, he was a young stud facing down a, to him, older man, and he wasn't about to back down.

Tough luck for him.

"I told you I got nothing to say to you, mister. I didn't answer any of your questions before, and I'm not about to answer them now."

"I disagree," I said.

"Huh?"

"I consider it very likely that you're going to tell me what I want. I'm not out to do you wrong, kid. I just need some information, then I'll be on my way."

His nostrils flared, probably at the "kid" comment. "Listen, old man. If you don't haul ass right now, I'm going to . . ."

I hit him. Not hard and nothing that would leave a mark. A short jab in the midsection.

Really, barely even a jab. I gave it to him no harder than I used to do back in the ring, when we usually pulled our punches.

Even so, it staggered him back and made him gasp. A moment later his shoulders tensed as if he was going to come at me again. I gave him a steely look in return, and after a heartbeat or two he took a step back.

"Okay," I said, "now that we've established who's on top, why don't we try this again. I'm not working for Laura's family, wouldn't know them if I passed them on the street. I can't tell you who I'm working for, but I can assure you no one's looking at you, not since the cops cleared you. I'm going down another trail altogether."

"What other trail?" he asked, the red slowly leaving his face.

"Can't tell you," I said. "But if you give me about ten minutes, I can practically guarantee you I'll head out the door and never bother you again."

"Practically guarantee?" he asked with what he no doubt hoped
passed for a tough grin.

"Far as I know. You going to invite me in now?"

Another moment of indecision on his part passed before he
stood aside and ushered me in.

Finally, down to business.

CHAPTER EIGHT

"**W**HAT IS IT YOU WANT TO KNOW?" Granger asked a moment later as I stepped into his house.

He didn't invite me to, but I went ahead and sat down, taking up one corner of a sagging, much-repaired couch. "Whose idea was it for you and Laura to break up?"

"Wow," Granger said, moving to stand in a corner of the room, his arms crossed. "I thought you said I wasn't a suspect anymore."

"You're not," I said, feeling like I'd been repeating myself all day. "Like I said, I'm pursuing another angle and need some background."

The kid thought about it for a minute. "What the hell. It's not like you couldn't find out from half a dozen of our friends. I broke up with her."

"Really?" I asked. "Pretty girl like her? What was the problem?"

Granger shuffled his feet and looked down at the floor. I got the impression he really wanted to sit down but no doubt figured he had to keep up the macho act as long as possible.

"Why do you think?" he finally said. His throat sounded a little tight.

"My first guess would be she was fooling around on you."

He chuckled, though it had a strained quality. "Fooling around? Really, man. How the hell old are you? I guess that's one way of putting it."

His arms crossed even tighter across his bare chest.

"Kid," I said, "why don't you sit down and let's talk things over man-to-man. I've got nothing to prove to you, and you've nothing to prove to me."

"Only because you sucker punched me a minute ago. If I'd been ready for it . . ."

"If you'd been ready for it, I would have hit you a whole lot harder and you'd still be down. I gave you a tap to get your attention, and it wasn't even remotely a sucker punch. Why not sit the hell down and get comfortable in your own house?"

He glared, tensed, and fumed for another minute or two before shaking his head once and collapsing into a brown leather chair to his left. "To hell with it," he muttered.

"That's better. So tell me what's wrong with saying fooling around?"

"Fooling around, as you put it, is when your girl takes up with another guy."

"Yeah?"

"Not when she takes up with fossils."

I tensed up a bit. "An older man?"

Granger shook his head and gave me a look as if to ask if I was the biggest dunce in the world. "I said fossils, as in plural."

Comes the light. "She had a thing for older men?"

Granger nodded. "Uh huh. The older the better, and the flashier the better. You think someone like me, in my twenties and working for hourly wages, can compete with guys with actual bucks? Or power? Or both? Not to mention who are old enough they don't, uhm, require a whole lot out of her?"

"You've got a pretty nice house here," I said.

"Got it when my dad passed away last year. He had it all paid off. Didn't leave much beyond that."

Which explained the rather thread-bare furniture.

"Know any names?" I asked, working to control my breathing.

"Not hardly, even though I tried like hell to find out. I suspected for quite a while she was messing around on me."

"Suspected how?" I asked.

Granger slitted his eyes my way. "I thought you were a private cop. Don't you know about this kind of stuff? Broken dates. Phone message or texts returned hours later. Suddenly begging off sick when I wanted to come over. After a while, it all adds up."

"I can see that," I said. "Never any clue as to any of their identities?"

"Nope. And it wasn't for lack of hassling her friends about it. But none of them would tell me a thing."

"You're pretty sure it was more than one?"

He thought about that one for a minute, staring off into space and slapping his thighs. After a while, he shook his head. "So maybe I was blowing off when I said that. I kind of had the impression she had one geezer in particular she was stringing along, but couldn't really say for sure."

"What kind of impressions?" I asked.

Granger shrugged and looked down at the floor. "Different people would tell me they spotted her driving around town with some guy, especially like a month before she died. I'd hear about her pulling up to places in limo's, with some dude trying to hide his face. Every now and then a girl who ran in our circle clued me in on Laura flashing some expensive jewelry. Only it wasn't all that expensive, you know? Like someone trying to impress her without being able to all the way."

"Just in the last month or so ?" I asked.

"Yeah, maybe only a few weeks before she got killed."

"You tell any of this to the cops?" I asked.

Granger snorted. "Tried to, but when we talked all they wanted to do was pin it on me and get it off their books. I tried two or three different ways to suggest they should track down whoever those guys were, but they were convinced I was the one they wanted."

"Until they checked out your alibi and saw that it was solid," I said.

Granger nodded. "I was actually out of town that weekend. Out of state, far as that goes."

"From what I heard," I said, "you were with some friends out in Colorado."

Granger bobbed his head up and down. "Bunch of us managed to throw enough bucks together to go in on a timeshare and do some skiing. Plus, Laura and I had been broken up so long I'm guessing they couldn't find any of my DNA around her place."

I refrained from shaking my head. Like most civilians who got all of their information from *Law and Order* reruns, Granger clearly had only the flimsiest notion of how DNA tracing actually worked.

"To recap, you know she was on the hunt for older guys. You don't know who and aren't sure how many," I said.

"That's pretty much it, man."

"And you think Laura's family isn't as convinced, right? Which is why you thought they hired me?"

"You sure they didn't?" Granger asked.

"Kid, I may be over the hill, but I'm pretty sure I can keep track of who my client is at any given time."

Granger stared down at the floor and dug his foot in for a second. "Okay, so maybe I overreacted when you showed up at work. It hasn't been easy, though, you know. Even some of my friends, not to mention Laura's, think I'm somehow involved. I'd just kind of like to put it all behind me."

Not the big tough-guy wannabe he'd first portrayed himself as. Just a young man, wanting to get on with his life after having a load of fertilizer dumped onto it. Figuring he'd told me everything he knew, or at least everything he knew he knew, I got up to leave.

I made a snap decision, then wondered if it would come back on Santiago in any way. At the moment it didn't really matter.

"Hang in there, Ryan," I said, my hand on the knob. "Tough it out a little longer, and trust me. Things are going to get better for you."

It was the closest I could come to letting him know the cops had another, much more attention-gathering, suspect in mind.

CHAPTER NINE

"**B**IG CASE, HUH?" TALIA SANDERSON ASKED me later that night.

"Uhm hmm." I stared down at the menu so as to avoid looking her in the eye. Talia, I'd discovered in our very short time of seeing each other, could sometimes peer right through me.

"Which, of course, you can't talk about," she said.

"No more than you can tell me about personnel issues at the university."

"True. But your job can sometimes be a lot more exciting than a college dean's."

"Not all that much," I said, eyes still glued to the menu. Though I'd already decided what I was going to order, I wanted to avoid her searching look.

"Let's change the subject then," she said. "Since you've already figured out what you're going to order, how about we call the waitress over here and get to it."

See what I mean about her being able to read me? I closed the menu and slid it over to the edge of the table. We were at a slightly upscale restaurant in downtown Providence. Not quite the kind of place that omitted putting prices on the menu, but one at which I had to budget for a week or so before entering.

Talia slid her menu over on top of mine, and I took a moment to gaze at her.

Talia's hair is a nice honey blonde which, though she's edging into her late forties, as far as I know she doesn't color. She has green eyes and, as more women are starting to do these days, wears her age very well. She keeps herself in shape, though without going overboard, and does nothing to hide the attractive laugh lines around her mouth.

This night, she was wearing a black, slimming sheath made of light cotton and black pumps, no hose. A thin gold chain dangled around her neck, and she'd had her hair cut short for the summer. With the basic school year over and her work duties slightly reduced, she was beginning to develop a honey-shaded tan.

My clean tee-shirt, linen sport coat, and two-day scruff of graying beard, made something of a contrast between the two of us.

Before I could begin drooling on the tabletop, our server showed up. "Decided?" she asked us.

I nodded in Talia's direction.

"I'll have the chicken piccata," she said, "and he'll take the black bean burger with extra fries."

Before I could say anything, the server, a cute little thing who probably spent her spare time practicing for the cheerleading team, glanced my way.

"What she said," I said, motioning to Talia.

The server nodded, picked up the menus and hurried off.

"I didn't want to make a scene in front of her," I said, "but what makes you think I wanted a black bean burger?"

"Maybe I just know you that well," Talia said.

"After only a few months?"

She grinned, and faint sparks showed up in those green eyes of hers. "Okay, then before I opened my big mouth, what were you planning to order?"

I grumbled something, pitching my voice low enough she couldn't catch it.

"Come again?"

"The black bean burger, alright?"

Her eyes sparkled even more.

"Don't be so giddy about a lucky guess," I said, trying to keep my face straight. "I'm still a man of mystery."

Talia laughed, so softly the people in the next booth probably couldn't hear. "Sure thing, man of mystery. I'll keep it in mind."

We indulged in small talk for a while until our food came, then spent several minutes in some serious chowing down, before she came back around to the question of the night.

"Can you say anything about it at all?" she asked.

"The case?" I asked as she nodded.

I shook my head. "Come on, Talia. You know better than that."

She smiled, somewhat impishly, and reached out to cover my hand with hers. "I know. I just wanted to make sure you were the same principled guy I met a few months ago."

"Not that principled," I growled, though I made no effort to move my hand from hers.

"It's pretty serious, huh?"

I nodded. "About as serious as it can get for a town this size. And that's all I can say about it."

"Okay, then. How 'bout we discuss something more immediate?"

"Immediate?"

"Yep," she said. "Like what's up next after this scrumptious meal you bought for me."

"I haven't a clue," I said.

"Hmm." She gave a pouty little frown. "Not such a good position for a detective to be in, no clues or anything."

"Maybe I'm not that good at my job," I said. "Care to give me any pointers?"

The impish smile again, verging on devilish, and I imagined if her superiors at the university could read her mind at the moment they'd be shocked at her impulses.

"Pointers," Talia said. "You bet, big fella. I've got pointers a-plenty for you."

CHAPTER TEN

THE NEXT MORNING, AFTER TALIA had left for the university, I was starting in on my first cup of coffee as I placed a call to the gym.

"Blaster," Lisa Nolan answered on the second ring.

"It's me," I said.

"What's up?"

"Just checking in to see how things been going the last few days," I said.

A slight pause before Lisa replied. "You been gone?"

Funny, I didn't know I'd hired a comedian. "I'll probably be back by first of next week or so. You need me for anything till then?"

"Not so far," Lisa said, "but I'll call if I do."

After we hung up, I stood there for a minute thinking. Competent as she was, I couldn't think of Lisa calling for anything short of an earthquake, and maybe not even then.

I picked up my phone again and made another call, this one to Lieutenant Santiago.

He answered on the second ring. "Hello?"

"Got a couple of questions for you," I said. The lieutenant hesitated, and I wondered if he was walking into another room to talk away from his wife, girlfriend, or kids. It occurred to me I knew nothing about the guy's home life, and I made a note to someday get the lowdown from Josh Nichols.

After all, pays to know your clients.

"Yeah?" he asked half a minute later.

"I talked to both the former boyfriend and Laura Mosby's boss. None of them seemed to know anything specific about the mayor, though the Granger kid did go on about how he suspected Laura was cheating on him with older men."

"Men as in plural?" Santiago asked.

"Yep. Though he also said that the last few weeks of her life he had the feeling there was one guy in particular she was catting around after."

A couple of seconds of dead silence before the cop spoke up again.

"Okay, so what's your question?"

"Actually, it's a couple. She lived alone, right?"

"Far as we could tell. Place only had stuff looked like it belonged to her, and no paper trail of anyone else living there, no extra name on the lease or utilities. Nothing even remotely suggesting a male tenant. And no one's come forward in all this time to say any different. You thinking she had someone in there with her?"

"Not that so much," I said. "I'd just like to get a track on who her best friend was."

"Best friend?"

"She had to have one. According to her boss, she didn't hang out much with the others at work, but Granger kept referring to their social circle and her friends. And did you ever know of a young lady who didn't have someone who she told all the juicy stuff too?"

"You're thinking whoever this best friend is, if anyone would know of a connection between the Mosby girl and the mayor, it would be her?"

"That's what I'm thinking," I said.

"Well, I can doublecheck with the detectives, but I haven't heard anything about any close friends. Don't recall anything in the interview notes I skimmed over either."

I thought about that through a couple sips of my coffee. "Is anyone still sitting on her place?" I asked.

"You mean in terms of surveillance? No. It's been a couple of months after all."

"Yeah, I know," I said. "She lived in a rental, right? You happen to know if the landlord's rented her place out yet?"

"Are you contemplating an illegal search by a private citizen?" Santiago asked.

"Would you want to know if I was?"

"Not hardly. The decision on whether or not to rent out her place wouldn't be the landlord's anyway. It would be the DA's."

"It would?" I asked.

"Yep. Sometimes, especially on something high-profile, they'll keep a place under wraps, in case it has to be revisited for some reason."

"You mean like how the OJ Simpson jury got to tour his house," I said.

"Like that. Though, way I recall it, his house had been gussied up quite a bit by the lawyers before the jury got there."

"Would the DA still have the place sealed up?" I asked.

"They would if they think they'd need it for a murder trial. They usually do their best to turn property over as soon as possible, but it doesn't always work that way."

"Can you find out for me whether they're still keeping her place tucked away?" I asked.

"Shouldn't be hard, though I'll have to do it quietly."

"Call me back," I said. "I'd like to look it over, and I don't want to home-invade some new tenant if I can avoid it."

"What if you can't find a best friend?" Santiago asked. "After all, my people went through there as thoroughly as possible, and they didn't find anything that's not listed in the reports."

"Then I go on to Plan B."

"Which is?"

I paused for a moment, choosing my words carefully. "Best you don't know, Lieutenant. You came to me because you needed some under-the-radar work, and for now the more we can keep it under the better."

I expected Santiago to fume a bit, at the least express some agitation. However, the man was a shrewd cop, and it only took him a second or two to see things my way. "Good point, for now.

If things get hairy, I need to be at least somewhat in the loop."

"Understood."

"Keep in mind, the main reason I brought you in is to protect my people. If something's going to cause any blowback—"

"I got you, Lieutenant. If anything starts to come down, you'll be the first to know."

"Give me fifteen minutes, tops," Santiago said, "and I'll get back to you about her place."

"Works for me," I said as I hung up.

CHAPTER ELEVEN

Laura Mosby had lived in a rented house on Greenway Street, tucked away in one of the small pockets of wooded areas that give Providence its unique appearance. It had taken Santiago little more than a quarter hour to determine from the DA's office that, yes, they had the house under seal until the investigation was completed and, not nearly as important to them, the landlord had threatened them with a lawsuit if they didn't relinquish the residence back to him.

The neighborhood formed a small cul-de-sac with eight houses forming the curve. Barely fifty feet from the outer curb of the sac loomed a patch of woodland, thick with intertwined trees all green in the summer sun, which no doubt housed any number of critters, including both deer and foxes.

Typical of the Providence scene. We have numerous pockets of dense, lush woods intertwined with residential and commercial areas.

I pulled up out front of the Mosby place and looked over the small, one-story dwelling with cracked, light blue paint and a dark green roof. While I couldn't tell for sure, it looked as if there was a bit of a cant to the house, as if something was going bad with the foundation. There was no fence, either for front or back, and what I could see of the lawn was trim and well-cared for.

An unattached garage, barely large enough to accommodate a Volkswagen Beetle, sat to the left, about seven feet from the house and with a flagstone walk connecting the two.

And despite the fact her murder had occurred months ago, fresh-looking crime scene tape decorated both the front door and the side doors of the house and garage.

No tape crisscrossed the main garage door, probably because that would have been a bit excessive even for Providence's DA.

The neighborhood itself appeared quiet on a summer day, leading me to think it was populated mainly by working adults. I didn't see any kids around, though in this day of streaming, MMP games, and general indoorsiness of youth, the quiet and solitude didn't exactly prove anything.

A block away, a middle-aged woman was walking a Great Dane. Other than that, I didn't see anyone else around.

Climbing out of the Cherokee, I walked up the driveway to the Mosby house, acting one hundred percent as if I belonged there. Had I been a television PI, I would have gone up to the front door, reached into my pocket for a set of lock picks, and had the door open in ten seconds at the max.

Seeing as how I don't own any lock picks, wouldn't have a clue how to use them if I did, and have been informed by people I trust that two-thirds of the time they don't work and the other third it can take something like ten minutes of effort before saying the hell with it and smashing the door open, I instead walked between the house and garage and headed to the back.

Despite the neighborhood appearing so empty, I moved as quickly as I could without coming off as suspicious to any lurking witnesses.

On the one hand, acting as if you belong in a particular place is about the best camouflage imaginable.

On the other, I generally look and move like an over-the-hill thug, and with police investigators being the only people who would have any legitimate reason nosing around the Mosby house, I saw no reason to push it.

I got a lucky break when I made it to the backyard. Despite the lack of fencing, a small stand of trees just back of the house provided halfway decent cover, meaning I could take a little more time as I examined the back door.

It had a fairly cheap lock, on a flimsy wooden door, and after putting on a pair of thin black gloves I looked both ways to make sure the coast was clear before putting my shoulder to it and popping it open. This caused a short screech as the door separated from its jamb. Rather than take the time to doublecheck if anyone had heard, I slipped inside and closed the panel behind me.

The average person, especially in a neighborhood like this, upon hearing an odd sound would no doubt glance outside, but seeing nothing out of the ordinary, such as a thuggish-looking middle-aged man prowling around, would more than likely shrug and go back about his business.

The layout of the house was about as I'd expected from the outside. Front living room, kitchen in the back, where I'd entered, with a thin wall partially separating the two. Hallway off the living room, three doors going off it, two on one side and one on the other. I assumed the three doors belonged to bedroom, smaller bedroom, and one bath.

The air in the house was thick and rather hard to breathe. Although early June, and with the weather not all that warm considering the time of year, the place had been shut up for a couple of months, and the atmosphere inside felt it.

I thought about opening a couple of windows to air things out, but didn't want to take the chance of someone passing by on the sidewalk and seeing me moving around. Instead, I took as deep a breath as I could and went about my business.

Fifty years ago, things would have been a lot easier. Back then, practically every young woman kept a dairy, or at least held on to letters, which could have given me all sorts of directions to pursue. Moving through the small house, I didn't see any computer, laptop, iPad or any similar device. I assumed, so much so I hadn't bothered to ask Santiago, that the cops had carted all that sort of stuff off.

So where to look for evidence of a close friend Laura Mosby may have confided in? I moved into the kitchen in the distant hope that, despite, her youth, she had had a landline phone, or at least some notes posted to the fridge.

No such luck.

The living room, what there was of one, contained a ratty blue couch, a worn green La-Z-Boy recliner, and a couple of bar stools. Way out of place was a 56-inch TV bolted to the west wall, along with three different remotes scattered across a coffee table badly in need of a good varnishing.

The worn-down atmosphere didn't really fit with the image in my head of an attractive young woman out for a good time. While young single people often don't have a whole lot in the way of accumulated material comforts, this seemed a bit much. Surely, she had made enough at the salon, especially when one included tips, to afford a little better than this.

Then I thought back to my own younger days living in St. Louis and working for the Midwest Wrestling League. Most people I knew casually assumed I was raking it in. They didn't seem able to distinguish between the wrestling stars who worked for major, national promotions and those who put on most of their shows in high school gymnasiums.

And in my youthful arrogance and pride, I often paid for far too many drinks and restaurant tabs in an attempt to live up to my acquaintances' perception of my lifestyle. All of that being one of the many reasons my wife and I had split up.

I stared at the TV for a moment, so out of place with the rest of the furnishings. A token from an older man? Some small thing to allow Laura to feel as if her life wasn't as shabby as it actually was?

Regardless, the living room didn't hold much of anything that could help me, which left only the obvious place to search, and with a deep breath I headed into the girl's bedroom.

According to both the news reports and what Santiago had shared, Laura Mosby had been found on her bedroom floor. That made the bedroom the central point of the investigation, and I had no doubt it had been tweezed, vacuumed, filtered, and combed until it said uncle.

And indeed, the room was pretty darned stark when I entered. Located towards the front on the east side of the house, the single window looked out to the garage. The rug, a pastel pink at one time but faded over time, still bore the chalked outline of the dead girl's body.

Okay, so I got that the DA wanted to keep the crime scene intact in case it became important at trial somewhere down the line, but this was getting a little ridiculous. Considering that, now months later, the cops didn't even have a viable suspect, at least as far as anyone knew, how long were they planning on keeping the house in stasis?

In terms of furniture, the room held only the iron frame of the bed, minus both mattress and box springs; a small nightstand up against the window; a battered old dresser; and a rickety white cane chair.

Against one wall, a small closet stood open with only a few blouses and slacks on hangars, a pile of faded blue jeans piled in a corner, and about twenty assorted pair of women's shoes.

Three hangars held outerwear: a lightweight cotton jacket and two heavy coats, one that looked like faux leather and one dark black wool, tattered around the cuffs.

A couple of small paintings, mainly of flowers, decorated the walls, and the dresser top held a couple of small jewelry boxes, along with a tiny glass vase that held three dead, dusty roses.

Even accounting for what the cops had no doubt taken out during their investigation, the bedroom reflected the living room in terms of not having much in the way of comfort or luxury.

It didn't even contain something wildly out of place, like the TV in the living room, to make Laura feel more comfortable in her personal space.

I riffled through the dresser first, finding nothing except the expected feminine clothing and accessories, then moved to check out the nightstand.

I didn't get there, though, because as I was about halfway across the room I saw the motion of a man-sized shadow outside the window.

I caught it only for a flick of an instant before it darted off to the side.

I froze, nearly holding my breath. I strained my middle-aged ears, and heard slight rustlings and creaks. Nothing that couldn't have, on an ordinary day, been the normal whispers of an old, decrepit house.

Moving as silently as possible, I moved to the wall next to the still-open bedroom door. As I hadn't expected any trouble, I didn't have a weapon with me, and I took a moment to flex and unflex my upper body, warming up for any possible action to come.

A minute later, I heard a slight click somewhere in the outer part of the house. It could have been a stray tree branch whipping against the kitchen window, or someone easing a door open and shut.

I began breathing again, short, shallow sips of air. Not quite enough to fully charge up my muscles, though better than nothing, and a damned sight better than gasping loud enough for someone to track me down.

Only then did I realize I'd parked right in front of the house. If, in fact, someone had entered, they had to know I was in there.

Okay, then. No chance of any real surprise, on either their end or mine.

Even so, I didn't want to charge through the doorway, yelling a banzai scream. I assumed whoever had entered, if in fact someone had and the shadow I'd seen hadn't been that of a passing car, was armed.

In other words, smarter than me, so why make things extra easy on them?

Several seconds went by without any noise, not even a stray wisp of air. It occurred to me the theoretical intruder, or intruders, could be cops making some sort of routine check on the property.

A moment after I had the thought, I discounted it. Especially if they thought someone was inside, cops wouldn't have been quietly sneaking around. They'd come in announcing themselves, making enough noise to flush any intruders out.

Okay, so scratch the cops. Who else would be skulking around a dead girl's house?

Her landlord came to mind. It would be a wild coincidence if, on the same day as I broke in to snoop around, he decided he'd had enough of waiting and wanted to clean the place out. It was possible, but a stretch.

Besides, as with cops, anyone with a legitimate reason to be in the house would have just come right in, rather than sneaking around.

Still no sound, no movement of any kind, and I began to wonder if the shadow I'd seen had just been some kid cutting through the yard.

Back to pondering as I continued to breathe slowly. If no one with a legitimate reason would be showing up here, then someone with an illegitimate one?

The ridiculous thought crossed my mind of the old cliché: the criminal returning to the scene of the crime. At first, I almost dismissed the idea as beyond stupid. Even if, for whatever reason, Laura Mosby's murderer would come back here, why months later? For what possible reason?

And why at this moment?

What was new about the case that would warrant him or her showing up?

The answer popped into my head almost immediately, and I felt a cold feeling in the pit of my stomach.

At the same instant, I heard the slight, high creak of door hinges come from the kitchen area.

Alright then, it hadn't been imagination, and it hadn't been some kid cutting across the yard.

Someone had entered the house, like me doing their best to keep their presence secret.

And I could think of only one reason why someone would have done so at this particular point in time.

Obviously, Santiago hadn't been as careful as he'd thought, and someone knew something about new information coming into the case.

And I had to clean up the mess.

CHAPTER TWELVE

I EASED MY WAY OUT OF THE BEDROOM. Although the house wasn't huge and didn't have a lot of room for action stuff, staying cornered in the room would have been the worst move to make.

Since I didn't know the intruder had a weapon, I had to assume he did. And since I didn't, I had to somehow get the jump on him before he could draw.

I was deliberately thinking only in terms of one man. There could just as easily have been two, three, or even more. But in circumstances like this, one was about all I could handle. If I was about to face a buddy situation, my chances of getting out in one piece would plummet, so I decided not to borrow trouble until I had to.

The noises from the kitchen had stopped, which meant either the intruder was standing stock still or that he could move without making a sound. I plastered myself against the hallway wall that angled towards the kitchen and began moving silently myself.

With my back against the wall, I did a kind of inverted crawl, lifting my left leg up, crossing it against the other, then doing the same with the right leg. About four movements like that had me at the corner angle, around which lay the kitchen.

This also put me within eyeshot of the living room, and a quick scan showed no one standing or sitting anywhere I could see.

My best hunch was the intruder still lurked in the kitchen, quite possibly having heard some slight noise from me. I got a mental image of him standing against the kitchen wall, parallel with me, both of us in the same position with only a thin layer of plaster-board separating us, each waiting for the other to make a move.

I began to feel a bit better that there was only one, mainly because had there been a team they would have already figured out a way to glom onto me. That left the only real question of whether or not the intruder had a weapon.

My legs began to cramp a bit, indicating the foolishness of standing around all day waiting for someone else to make a sloppy move, at the same time they were no doubt standing around waiting for the same thing.

Basically, then, it came down to which of us had the most patience.

Or was more professional.

In the next instant, I knew the answer.

A ring tone, some indefinable pop music lyrics from the nineties, chirped out briefly from just around the kitchen corner. Next came the slightest rustle of clothing, no doubt as the person on the other side reached into a pocket to silence his phone.

Even so, the damage was done, meaning the time had come to make a move.

Taking a deep breath in anticipation, not in fear (or so I told myself), I whipped around the corner and into the kitchen, as I did so colliding with the form on the other side, a tall, lean black man, who it appeared had indeed been carbon copying my moves.

In the next instant, as he grabbed me in a bear hug and tried to tackle me to the floor, I let out that breath in relief. Had the fellow had a gun he would have used it, making the two of us at least on more or less equal footing.

The only problem was, at the moment, I couldn't figure out where I came out on the more or less side of the equation. Although it was hard to tell tussling around the way we were, I had the impression the dude had a good couple of inches on me in height. And while with my extra weight, most of it still muscle at my age, that shouldn't have been much of a problem, I was finding it rather difficult to get a good lock on him.

He hooked his left leg behind my right, sending me crashing to the cracked linoleum floor. While that was bad for me, it wasn't too good for him either, seeing as how I managed to keep my grip around him as we went down. I felt a twinge in my back as we hit the ground, then ignored it as I tightened the hug, hearing his ribs start to creak beneath my arms.

His face began to turn a little purple as I squeezed even tighter. He started flipping his head back and forth, probably attempting to get underneath my chin so he could give me a good bonk. Ducking my chin against my breastbone, I squeezed even tighter.

Back in the old days, The Blond Bomber was known for the power of his bearhugs. 'Course, back then my opponent was going along with me, which made looking like a tough guy a whole lot easier.

Not so easy when the other dude's actually fighting back.

He began squirming his legs back and forth, and I had the idea he was attempting to get some leverage to give me a good knee in the groin. Not liking that idea so much, and beginning to get a little out of breath and arm weary, I figured the time had come to put him down.

Still under the intruder, I did a quick shift to the right, as I did so flipping my upper body in a way that sent him crashing to the floor, his head banging on the linoleum.

Although the move didn't knock him out, it rang his bell enough to loosen his grip, giving me the opportunity to scooch back just enough to give me some room to make a move, which I did.

The move being a solid left hook to his chin. The guy's eyes rolled up in his head for a flash before coming back down, and while once again he wasn't all the way out, by this time he was clearly not in the mood for any more action.

He wore a thigh-length black leather blazer. In the summertime, no less. I pulled one of the oldest tricks in the book by flipping him over onto his stomach, then yanking the blazer halfway down his arms, effectively pinioning him. Would have worked better if the jacket had been buttoned, but you take what you can get.

Then, flipping him back onto his back, I knelt over him and raised my fist up for another blow.

"All right, man, you made your point," he said in a deep, slightly hoarse voice. He probably would have raised his hands if they weren't already pinioned and I hadn't been half sitting on him.

Before letting him up, I did a quick frisk to make sure he wasn't armed. Doing so, I came across an ID wallet in his inside jacket pocket. One that looked suspiciously like the one I carry. He lay quiet as I flipped the wallet open and looked inside.

"Satisfied?" he asked, again with that slight trace of hoarseness.

"For now." I stood up and moved a few feet away, motioning him to get up.

He stood, took off his leather blazer and brushed off any dirt that had accumulated from our scuffle. Then he put the jacket back on and looked my way. "I'm not a crook, if that's what you're thinking."

"It had crossed my mind," I said.

"Probably thought I was just breaking in?"

"Maybe," I said, "though you don't fit the usual smash and grab profile."

He stared at me for a moment, and I got the impression he made up his mind about something. "James Ericson," he said, holding out his hand, "but you know that already from my ID, right?"

I braced myself, then relaxed, figuring if I took him once I could take him again.

"Sam Quinton," I said, taking the offered hand.

"Maybe we should go somewhere and talk."

"Maybe we should," I said.

CHAPTER THIRTEEN

We ended up at a hole-in-the-wall bar about ten minutes away. I'd suggested the place, and James Ericson had agreed. We took separate cars. His, a silver Corvette convertible, parked about two blocks away from Laura Mosby's house. I could either trust him to show up or we'd go another round, probably something neither of us felt like doing.

He actually got to the bar a minute or two ahead of me, and we sat down in a front booth that looked out the front of the building. It was a moderate little place, more of a neighborhood establishment than anything else. Set in the middle of a small strip mall, that early in the afternoon we were the only two customers in the place.

Feeling generous, I went up to the bar, got two bottles of beer and brought them back to the table.

"How about cards on the table?" Ericson suggested as I sat down and slid one of the bottles over to him.

Nodding, I pulled out the photostat of my PI license and plopped it in front of him. He looked it over for a moment.

Smiling, he slid my license back to me. "Looks like we're in the same business, Quinton. Even if you're a lot more local than me."

"Maybe," I said, "although Rolla's not exactly the far side of the moon." Rolla, a town of about twenty thousand or so people, lay a hundred miles or so south of Providence.

"True."

"Has me curious, though. Why someone from out of town was hanging around Laura Mosby's place."

"You asking who my client is?"

"Well, yeah, actually I am."

"Glad to tell you. Just as soon as you tell me who yours is."

I paused. Professional courtesy notwithstanding, no way in hell could I blab about Santiago hiring me. Even if I didn't go into any more detail than that, the very notion of a police official hiring a private license off the books would lead to all sorts of speculation.

At the very least, it was something Ericson would feel obligated to pass on to his client.

"Of course," I said, "your client could be the girl's family. According to the ex-boyfriend, they're not all that happy with him."

"Could be," Ericson replied. "Would kind of make sense, wouldn't it? After all, it has been a couple of months with no progress by the cops."

"True, but there's a little problem with that theory."

"Which is?"

"She grew up, and her family still lives, in Ohio. Wouldn't they either hire someone locally here, or at the very least, someone they knew from back home?"

Ericson grinned. "Possibly. Then again, maybe I'm just that good."

"Could be, but doubtful."

Ericson's grin widened. "Who'd you say you were working for again?"

I shook my head, and we both took a moment to drink our drinks.

"So where do we go from here?" Ericson asked as he placed his half-drained bottle down.

"Maybe we figure out what we can tell each other," I said.

"Such as?"

"What you were looking for in Laura's house."

He leaned back in the booth, his grin having now turned into a smirk. "Guess I could ask the same of you, couldn't I?"

"We just going to keep playing games like this? You know I could call the cops and clue them in on your little B&E. That may put the brakes to your investigation pretty quick."

The smirk now turned into a full-blown smile, which threatened to split his face in half. "Wouldn't take me long to point out to the police how it is you knew about my—ahh—breaking into her place. Besides, if I'm working for the fam, I'd say I had a little more right to be there than you."

I didn't want to give him the pleasure of watching me plunk my head on the table in realization of how I'd walked into that one, but I almost couldn't help myself. A strategic retreat seemed in order.

"Tell you what," I said, "why don't we see how much info we can share with each other without actually saying anything."

"Sounds like an idea. You start."

"Even if the family wanted to hire an outside investigator, I would guess it would be either someone local or that they knew personally."

Ericson tapped his fingers on the table a few times before nodding. "I'd say that's a safe assumption."

"The family's been carrying on almost constantly about the old boyfriend. But considering that the cops were all the way through her house months ago, it's very slim there'd be anything there to link Granger to her death. Otherwise, they'd have him up on charges."

"So?"

"So I'm guessing your little—excursion—today has nothing to do with any vendetta against the boyfriend."

Ericson nodded, his smile a bit more genuine now. "You're not bad, Quinton. Though you're still a puzzle."

"Oh yeah?"

"Yeah," he mimicked my tone, "and don't act all mysterious. I got the full scope on this case before I came up here, which means I'm still puzzled as to your involvement."

"Maybe I have an overriding desire to see justice done," I said.

"Maybe. Or it could be you have an overriding desire to bullshit an out-of-towner. I'm going to assume neither is true, and that you have an actual honest-to-goodness client paying you to snoop around."

"Could be."

"Which leaves the question of who. As you've said, the Mosby girl's family lives out of state, and besides which, from what I understand, this whole time her mom's been the only one really raising hell. And considering the girl's age, I don't see you and her as close friends or anything, which leaves out the personal angle. So your whole deal here is a bit of a puzzle." Ericson leaned back and took a long draft of his beer.

"Gets me back to the question of who, in your neck of the woods, would have any interest in this case," I said.

"Could be all sorts of people," he replied. The guy had really missed his calling. Instead of detective work, he should be in Vegas or Atlantic City playing poker professionally.

"Far as I know," I said, "Laura Mosby didn't have any connections down there."

Ericson took another drink, his mug now almost empty. "Far as you know. Again, though, I'm sitting here thinking the same things. If not the girl's family, who would be hiring a PI to look into her killing? It's not like she was important or anything."

There was a little glint in his eye, one he couldn't quite conceal, and something clicked in my head.

As far as I knew, Mayor Marlow didn't have any business interests outside of politics. And for sure no connections to Rolla I knew of, though I would make sure to check that out later. However, I could see one possible reason why someone from about a hundred miles away would be interested in checking out the murder of a young woman in Providence.

I raised my mug to drink, thinking as quickly as I could. I didn't want to give anything away that would screw up Santiago's case down the line, but I had a wild card sitting here in front of me, and I had to make a snap decision as to how to proceed.

"Well, this has been fascinating," Ericson said after draining the rest of his glass, "It seems like we're not about to trust each other or anything, and I do have things to be doing, so—"

He stood up to leave. As he slipped on his leather blazer, I decided to go for it.

"See you around, Ericson," I said.

The black detective grinned down at me. "Maybe, maybe not, Quinton. Take care of yourself."

He straightened up, and as he turned to leave, I made my move.

"Tell me, Ericson. How's the political weather down your way?"

He paused, then turned back to me. He started to say something, then changed his mind and instead held up his hand and shot me with his finger.

Then he left me pondering this new element in the case.

CHAPTER FOURTEEN

I EXITED THE BAR A MINUTE AFTER ERICSON, waiting until I was in the driver's seat of the Cherokee before I pulled out my phone and placed a call to Santiago.

He answered on the third ring. "Yeah?" he mumbled. I could hear other voices in the background.

"Can you talk?" I asked.

"Hold on." Another round of mumbling, then what sounded like a door shutting before he spoke up again. "Okay, what's up?"

"Did I interrupt something important?"

"Regular weekly meeting of department heads." Over the phone, I could almost visualize the lieutenant's annoyed grimace.

"On a Wednesday afternoon?" I asked. "Aren't those things usually held at the beginning or end of the week?"

"Usually Monday morning first thing. But the chief just got back from a week of skiing somewhere, so it's today. What's up?"

"We may have a problem." I filled him in on my meeting and heart-to-heart chat with James Ericson.

"Shit," was the lieutenant's pithy response.

"Yeah. That's about what I thought. But for some reason, it's ringing a bell. Why do I think Rolla has some connection with the mayor? He from there or something?"

"Not that I know," Santiago said. "You've obviously got your phone with you. Why didn't you check it out before calling me?"

I grinned. "Didn't want you to think my job was too easy."

"Meaning you bug me instead of checking it out yourself?"

My grin eased away. "Man, didn't think that through, did I? But you're more tuned into the local power structure than I am. Any idea what the connection could be?"

"Give me a minute." Santiago said. As I waited, I looked out of the parking lot at a tan Dodge Charger, several years old, parked down the street, about four car lengths from the entrance to the parking lot. Though I couldn't tell for sure, it looked like the body had little specks of rust here and there.

Two people were sitting in the front seat of the Charger, in the middle of the day, and I began to get an odd feeling in my gut.

"Nope," Santiago eventually came back on the line. "Nothing connecting Marlow to Rolla, or anywhere around that area."

"What about Laura Mosby? She have any family or anything down there? Live there for a while? Anything?"

"I'm going by memory here," Santiago said, "but not that I remember. Reynolds and Krenshaw would have a clearer idea on that."

"Too bad I can't walk up and ask them," I said, my eyes still on the Charger down the road. "So why does a small town a hundred miles down the road suddenly factor into this case?"

A couple of moments of silence passed between the two of us before Santiago finally broke it.

"Damned if I know," he said.

"Yeah," I replied. "Same here."

CHAPTER FIFTEEN

Santiago and I talked for another few minutes without making much more headway. After we hung up, I started up the Cherokee and pulled it out of the parking lot and onto the street, heading in the opposite direction of the tan Charger.

Sure enough, the Charger pulled out behind me, and they were gracious enough to let me get around the corner before flashing the red and blue lights to pull me over.

I did so, turning the ignition off, placing my hands in plain sight on the wheel and waiting for the cops to come get me.

For a minute, we just sat there, the cop car pulled in behind me close enough I could make out the two people, a man and a woman, occupying the front seats. Far as I could tell, they weren't doing anything except maybe talking. No use of the radio, no polishing up of brass knuckles to knock me around with, nothing.

Could be that below the window line they were dividing the spoils from some small-time retailer they'd just shaken down. Somehow, I doubted it.

After four or five minutes, both doors opened, and the two got out and walked up to my vehicle, one on each side. Even before exiting their car, I'd pretty much guessed who they were.

The man, an average-sized guy in his early forties, was wearing a tan suit with a light blue shirt and red tie, about as basic a wardrobe as you could get. He tapped on my window. I rolled it down and, out of consideration for his partner, rolled down the passenger side window at the same time.

"Good afternoon," the man said. "How are you doing today?"

"Doing fine, Matt," I replied. "Haven't seen you around the gym lately."

Detective Matt Reynolds, a senior investigator in Santiago's unit, stiffened and sent a quick glance in his partner's direction. The woman, young, slender, with blonde hair and blue eyes, had a bit more fashion sense than her partner. She wore white denims and a light-yellow sleeveless blouse. Unlike female cops on TV and the movies, she had black running shoes on her feet.

She didn't wear a blazer, leaving her holstered weapon conspicuously clipped to her left hip. She kind of reminded me of a TV cop I'd been watching on a streaming series a few years back.

The woman stared at me with a frozen look. I got the impression Reynolds hadn't mentioned to her that we knew each other.

"I've been busy, Sam," Reynolds said. "You know how it is."

Nodding, I kept his partner in my peripheral vision. "Makes sense. Though if you're so busy, why are you pulling me over?"

"Well, Sam, we've got a problem here."

"Hopefully, one we can work out."

"I hope so too."

"Oh for God's sake, Matt," the woman interjected. "Stop dicking around with him."

Reynolds sighed and shook his head at me. "Sam, this is Detective Abbie Krenshaw. She's a transfer. Arrived in town from Oklahoma City last year. She and I are partnered up at the moment."

"I figured as much," I said, "but I'm still waiting to hear what's going on."

"It's like this," Reynolds said, "a little while ago we got a report of a pearl cashmere Cherokee hanging out in a suspicious manner in a residential area. When we ran plates and description, guess what we found?"

"I'm guessing you found that the vehicle in question belonged to me. Sounds like damned good police work that you managed to track me all the way here from a random."

"It's what we do. Track people down. How about it?"

"If you're referring to the neighborhood I think you are, seems to me what you call acting suspiciously someone else could call being parked on a public street. So what's the big deal?"

"Here's the big deal, Mr. Quinton," Krenshaw spoke up. I turned to face her full on. "You were spotted hanging around an active crime scene. Considering your occupation, you can imagine that raised all kinds of flags."

I took a deep breath, giving myself time to think. "How active of a crime scene can it be, Detective, if the case is over two months old?"

"Come on, Sam," Reynolds said. "Abbie has a point. Tell us straight up, okay? What were you doing hanging around the girl's place?"

It occurred to me they hadn't asked anything about James Ericson, which could mean everything or nothing.

"You've got people surveilling her house?" I asked.

"It doesn't matter what we've got," Krenshaw said. "For the last time, just answer the damned question."

"Laura was behind on some furniture payments," I said.

Reynolds grimaced, and Krenshaw exhaled in disgust.

"You doing repo work now, Sam?" Reynolds asked. "Things must be tough all around."

"Just doing a favor for a friend," I said.

"What's the store's name?"

"Do I have to tell you that?" I asked.

"Oh for God's sake." Krenshaw's hand drifted down below the window frame, and I wondered if she were about to pull her gun out. "Come on, Matt. Can't you tell the guy's jerking you around?"

Reynolds stood up a little straighter. "Of course I can, Detective. And seeing as how you only got that shield six months ago, why don't you step back a moment and let me handle this?"

If looks could scorch, Reynolds would have been nothing but a pile of ash on the ground. Even so Krenshaw, her lips compressed into a single line, took a step back and relaxed her posture.

"Okay then," Reynolds said, locking eyes with me. "Doesn't matter how long ago the girl died, Sam. A crime scene's a crime scene until decided otherwise, and it's not up to a private license to do the deciding. Got it?"

"I got it, Matt."

"You didn't go inside, did you?" he asked.

"You think I'd go that far?"

"Knowing you," said Reynolds, "you'd go as far as you think you needed to. And why don't we drop the whole 'repo' angle. Did you take anything out of the house?"

Still no indication they'd spotted Ericson. Although I didn't dare ask, my best guess was they had the Mosby place on a list for patrol cars to do periodic drive byes. If so, considering that Ericson had been parked farther down the street, they'd missed him. One of those periodic sweeps had probably happened while we were inside the house, and shortly after it had been called in, the detectives had come a calling.

Since the bar Ericson and I had ended up at was only a short distance from the Mosby house, wouldn't have been too hard to spot me.

Overall, because there was a good chance they didn't even know for sure I'd been in the place, I decided not to push my luck. At the moment, staying on their right side seemed the better part of valor.

"No, Matt. I didn't take anything. Just did a look around to get the lay of the land, so to speak."

Reynolds nodded while Detective Krenshaw snorted. "You're not going to take this guy's word for that, are you?" she asked her partner.

Reynolds looked past me to glare at the younger cop. "Considering he could have denied being in the house at all, I think we can."

"But—"

"Can it, Abbie. Sam and I go back a ways, and I say he's clean. At least for now."

"From what I hear, half the department would say he's clean."

"What about the other half?" I asked.

"You really want to know?" Krenshaw said with such a deadpan face I couldn't tell if she was joking or not.

"Okay, Sam," Reynolds brought my attention back to him. "Whatever you're doing, I'm guessing it's more or less within the lines of the law. Even so, the Mosby place is off limits from now on. Got it?"

"Roger that, Matt. And thanks for being so gracious about this."

Reynolds cracked a grin. "I have to be decent about it. The alternative is to bracelet you up and haul you downtown, and judging by Krenshaw's expression there, I seriously doubt we'd get more than halfway there before she pulled her piece and put you out of my misery."

"And you wouldn't want that on your conscience, right?"

The cop shook his head, the grin intact. "Forget conscience, man. You think I want to deal with all the paperwork?"

"So I'm free to go?" I asked.

"You are if Krenshaw there will step away from your car and let you drive off."

I glanced over at Providence's newest detective. She glared at both of us for a second before stepping back and crossing her arms. I smiled at her, which she didn't return, then decided to cut my losses.

"See you around," I said.

"Hopefully not around any more crime scenes, Sam. Keep it cool. You hear?"

"I hear. Good to meet you, Detective." I nodded in Krenshaw's direction as I fired up the engine and headed off.

I could feel her glaring all the way until I turned a corner and got out of sight.

CHAPTER SIXTEEN

GREAT, NOW I HAD SANTIAGO'S PEOPLE dogging me without knowing we were, more or less, on the same side. As I drove away, I thought it over and after a minute realized it probably wouldn't be all that bad of a deal. After all, I only had a short time to gather whatever I could before Reynolds and Krenshaw got a look at the DNA report and figured out they had a lot bigger problem than they were currently aware of.

Which made it even more crucial I get my own act into gear and start doing what Santiago had hired me for.

Coasting up to a stop light, I pulled my phone out and placed a call to a friend of mine. We hadn't spoken in a couple of years, but I was sure she'd still have my number saved.

"What the hell do you want, Quinton?" Though the words were harsh, the voice had a bit of a chirp to it.

Yep, she still remembered.

"Hi, Angie. It's been a while, so I wanted to check in and see how you're doing."

There was a slight pause before she answered, and I heard the sound of computer keys tapping.

"It's been more than a while, and all things considered I've actually been doing okay. So what does my favorite ex-jock want?"

"Come on, Angie. Can't I call an old friend up out of the blue and say hi?"

"I'm not entirely sure that 'friends' is the best description for us, even back then."

"That hurts."

"Can't stand the heat and all that, Quinton. What do you want?"

"Remember the days when you used to call me Sam?" I asked.

"Sure. Practically every time I eat raw fish. And I'm on a deadline, so either tell me what you want or hang up."

Angela Tickman's a reporter for our one and only daily paper. For the last five years, she'd covered the local politics, primarily City Hall, beat.

"What I'd like," I said, "is to take you to dinner."

"Chuck E. Cheese or Taco Bell?"

"We don't have a Chuck E. Cheese in town anymore," I said. "And instead of Taco Bell how about food we can both keep down."

Angie stayed silent for a minute or so, the only sound the tapping of her fingers on her desk. "Why the sudden interest in my nutrition?" she asked.

"Because I need some information, and you're the most discreet person I know who can help me."

"You think I'm discrete because I haven't blabbed around town about how we broke up?"

"There's that. But I also know that, unlike a lot of people in your profession, you only print what you can verify."

"Meaning what?"

"Meaning I'm interested in some stuff you may know but don't have any backup for."

Another round of tapping, this time only for a few seconds. "Tell you what, Quinton, I could stand a good meal. You up for Italian?"

"You mean pizza Italian or the kind of Italian that will put me behind in my rent?"

"If the info you want is important enough to call me up and do the old times sake thing, sounds like it would be worth taking a chance on."

I sighed, hoping Santiago would come through with his voucher, and we set up a time and place for later that evening.

CHAPTER SEVENTEEN

ANGIE TICKMAN AND I HAD HAD A BRIEF FLING a couple of years back. We'd met when she came in to interview me for a story. At the time, she was taking a break from covering politics and was researching a fluff lifestyle piece on local workout facilities. I was one of about seven gym and health club owners she'd profiled, and when I suggested she may want to do a separate story on a former wrestler turned gym owner and private eye, she'd laughed and said no one would believe it.

So much for my one shot at fame.

Even with that shootdown, we'd hit it off a bit, and a couple of weeks later she called up to clarify a few meaningless pieces of information for her story. I'd figured out real quick what she was angling for and cut her off at the pass by asking her out first. She'd agreed, we'd gone to a show that weekend, and after continued to see each other.

Although we'd had a few laughs and gotten along okay, it was one of those things you knew almost from the get go wasn't really going anywhere, and after a few months we'd mutually decided to call it quits. About the same time, she felt rejuvenated after her sort of sabbatical, and to her editor's delight had returned to the local politics beat.

While Providence isn't exactly the nexus of political intrigue in the Midwest, we've got enough of a good ole' boys (and gals) network going on that some juicy stuff occasionally comes to light.

Angie was good at her work; she was fair; and if she told you something you could trust it all the way.

Turns out she showed a little mercy on me in that her choice of Italian eateries, while not exactly fast food, also wouldn't force me to take out a new mortgage on The Blaster to pay for our meal. When I got to the small restaurant, tucked away in a little side street squarely between our downtown area and the university campus, she was already sitting at a table, furiously punching away on a small tablet.

Angie Tickman is the only person I know who could literally punch a tablet.

When I'd met her a few years back, she'd been a fairly petite five foot four. She'd had auburn hair cut severely short, and usually wore jeans and tee-shirts, which made the two of us a perfectly-matched couple.

The woman sitting at the table in front of me bore some resemblance to the Angie from back then, though a little older, more mature, and, along with that, more attractive. The hair was now shoulder length and slightly curled at the tips. Basically the same auburn color, but with a touch of gray here and there, and while it was hard to tell with her sitting down, she seemed to have added about fifteen pounds or so that rounded out her figure in a good way.

Up close, I could see a couple of lines in her face I didn't remember from before, which once again enhanced her looks.

She also had a pair of probably the darkest brown eyes, almost black, I've ever seen.

She wore a black silk blouse opened a couple of buttons to display a gold pendant around her neck.

I suddenly felt like an old lug compared to her.

"Work not over for the day?" I asked as I sat down in the seat facing hers. Angie looked up, gave me a half smile, then bent back down to her tablet.

I was remembering one of the reasons I wasn't heartbroken when we stopped seeing each other.

I waited patiently for her to get done with her task, whatever it was. Only took a couple of minutes before she grinned, punched one last thing, and put the device away in the black leather purse slipped over one side of her chair back.

"You look good, Quinton," she said, her use of my last name making it clear that, even if I'd come with such intentions, anything smacking of romance was off the menu.

"You're holding up pretty well yourself, Angie," I said as a waiter, seeing both seats now occupied, came over with glasses and menus.

"And all without using a gym," she said, grinning, as we both bent over the menus.

"Still hiking the trails?" I asked. In the past, Angie had been obsessive about spending time on the various woodland paths that wend their way through Providence and the surrounding area.

"As often as I can."

We did some obligatory small talk, Angie talking about how hard it was to keep going at a newspaper in the modern digital world and me bringing her up to speed on how well the gym was doing. By unspoken mutual consent, we stayed away from inquiring about each other's personal lives.

After about five minutes, Angie got to it. "So what do you need from me?"

I had to hold off a minute as the server came by and took our food and drink order, and once the young girl walked off I got right to it.

"First off," I said, "this is off the record."

"Okay."

"I mean really off the record, Angie. I'm looking for hard info, but if I can't get that I'll take feelings, vibes, even gossip. The kind of stuff you know but couldn't ever put into print without risking a slander suit."

"Libel," Angie corrected me. "Slander is spoken defamation, libel is written."

I nodded and took a long drink of water. "Either way, we need it clear up front."

"Sounds like you're really biting at something."

"Clear or not, Angie? All the way off the record."

She paused for a moment as one of the wait staff brought our salads. The young man walked away, and we spent a few minutes digging in.

"What's in it for me?" Angie asked, putting down her fork for a minute.

"Potentially, first crack at a story like this city, hell this state's, never seen."

"Potentially?"

I nodded. "It may be nothing. I may be barking up a completely dead tree. If I am, there's no story. Not even the hint of one. I don't want to ruin anyone's life with unfounded speculation. But if I'm right, it could be the biggest thing in your career."

"You mean I'm taking a gamble that I'll provide you what you want, and it may or may not come to anything?"

Before I could answer, the server came by again and placed our plates, linguini for Angie and scampi for me, in front of us. Steam actually rose up from the plates, and my mouth began to water.

"That's basically the deal," I said when we were again alone. "You interested?"

Angie took a bite of her pasta and spent longer than necessary chewing it, no doubt giving herself time to think things over. "Well," she said, putting down her fork, "by nature I'm not a risk-taker, though I did go out with you a couple of times."

"Which may show not so much risk-taking as good taste," I said.

She smiled, her eyes lighting up a little in the half light of the restaurant. "Maybe, but that's all under the bridge, so to speak. However, in the short time we hung around each other, I never knew you to be deceitful, so what the hell. I'll take your deal."

"Thanks, Angie, but I need to emphasize. Anything you dig up for me, if I say no go, then it's no go. You can't go to the cops, or anyone else. Me alone or not at all."

Her eyes flickered, and for a moment I thought she was going to change her mind. Then she nodded and took another bite of linguini.

I celebrated my minor victory by digging into my dinner, and it more than satisfied my watering mouth. After a few minutes of the two of us masticating, Angie put down her fork again and looked up at me, the mirth gone from her eyes and her gaze all business now.

"So," she said, "what is it you want to pump me about?"

I glanced around to make sure no one was close enough to hear anything.

"Bob Marlow," I said.

"The mayor? You want me to spill the beans on the man who may be the next governor?"

"Are there beans to spill?"

"How much time you got?" Angie asked.

Uh huh. The look in her eyes told me I may have just hit a jackpot.

CHAPTER EIGHTEEN

"**A**NY PARTICULAR AREA OF INTEREST YOU HAVE?" Angie asked about an hour later.

In order to ensure privacy, we'd finished our meal, then gone to her place to talk business. Angie had moved since the last time I'd seen her, and the little rental house on the south side of town looked to be a step down from the apartment she'd had before. When we'd first walked inside, she must have read my mind from my expression.

"'What do you think?" she asked, her tone challenging.

The living room had minimal furnishings. A maroon three-seater couch squared off with two easy chairs, one done in red cloth and one a straight-backed rocker. On opposite walls were a small red-brick fireplace and a forty-inch television bolted to the wall. All of this on bare, hardwood floors.

"Looks nice, but your old place was a lot closer to the action."

"You mean less domestic?" She grinned as she threw her purse on the coffee table. "Maybe. Having a luxury apartment in the heart of downtown may seem like the nice life, except for the nine months out of the year when all the college students are in town, carousing up and down the sidewalk outside your window at all hours. Not to mention the rent downtown costs over a thousand a month for one bedroom."

Nodding, I took my coat off and slung it over the rocker. Angie gestured me to have a seat, and I plopped myself onto one end of the couch. She offered me something to drink, got us both bottles of beer, then came in and took the other couch end.

"Actually, I am interested in one thing in particular," I said. "And that's the good mayor's social life."

Angie look a long drink before putting her bottle down on a sunflower-decorated coaster. "I'm sure you know he's a happily married man," she said with a slow drawl.

"I assumed as much." I drawled out my response even slower than hers. "The question is, what is it keeps him happy?"

Angie gave me a slanted eye. "You moving on from criminal stuff, Quinton? Heading into divorce work? Or maybe insurance, checking out sexual harassment claims?"

"There anything there to check out?'

She took another drink, a longer one this time. I still hadn't touched mine.

"Not really," Angie said when she finally came up for air. "You may recall a couple of years ago we had a certain governor who got into a little trouble with that kind of thing."

"I do recall."

"So it wouldn't make a lot of sense for someone who wants to fill the same chair to make the same sort of mistakes."

"At least publicly," I said. "I'm sensing a but coming up, Angie."

Grinning, she placed her bottle back down, leaned back against the cushions, crossed her arms behind her head, and gave her eyes a bit of slit. "Let's just say that in the past, Marlow's been careful not to crap too close to where he eats."

"In the past?"

"Uhm hmm." Still the slitted eyes.

My breathing slowed a bit, and I began thinking about a certain PI from down south I'd recently met.

"Why don't we assume I'm more interested in the present. He still keep his distance?"

Angie craned her neck and stared at the ceiling for a moment before looking back down at me. "You've got me curious as hell, Quinton. Why don't you stop monkeying around and ask what you want to know?"

"Does the mayor fool around?" I asked. I felt a bit embarrassed when I remembered how Ryan Granger had sneered at the old-fashioned term.

Angie snorted, somehow making it sound dignified. "Fool around? Of course, he does."

"Does his wife know?"

"Unless she's both blind and deaf. How many times does the mayor of a town this size have to go away on business?"

"You know this for a fact?"

"One hundred percent. I've talked to a couple of the girls here and there, way on the downlow. It's been going on for years, but he's low-key enough that outside of one or two of his aides, and the girls themselves, he keeps it fairly quiet."

I thought that one over for a minute. When the colleges aren't in session, Providence has a population of a little over one hundred thousand. Marlow had been mayor for almost two full terms, having easily won re-election the first time around. If he'd been stepping out for even half that time, it seemed almost impossible for it not to be the worst kept secret in town.

"You've never printed anything about it," I pointed out. "Your decision or your editor's?"

Angie took another swig from her bottle. "My call. I haven't even discussed it with editorial. Each time I'd hear a whisper, I looked into it, but couldn't find any way in which his—activities— played a role in his job. He does a pretty good job of keeping the two separate. Plus, far as I've ever been able to tell, nothing illegal and nothing that would open up the city to any kind of litigation."

"Christ, Angie. Are you sure you're a reporter?"

She beamed at me. "So sue me. I've got an old-fashioned sensibility."

"Or maybe you're just stockpiling info for when it becomes relevant," I suggested. "Any of your compatriots in town know about this?"

"I'm sure they do, but you have to understand, Quinton. Have you ever met His Honor?"

"Never had the pleasure," I said.

"If you had, you'd get the picture. It doesn't quite come across when you see him on snippets of news at city council meetings, but he's as good ole' boy as one can get. Not sure, but I think he grew up somewhere down in the Ozarks. You take one look at him, and you can just tell he hits on anything that catches his fancy."

"Isn't that a little out of fashion these days?" I asked. "Lots of people have gotten in trouble for that attitude the last few years."

Angie shook her head and smiled at my naivete. "The more things change."

"Even so, you've been keeping an eye on him, right?"

Her beaming almost blinded me now. "You going to give me any nuggets I can use at all?"

"No," I said. "I'm afraid you'll use them."

She gave me a pout then, though more of a play pout than the real thing. "You really do have something you're tracking down on him, don't you?"

"Maybe," I said, "and maybe not. I guarantee if anything does float to the surface, you'll get the heads up first."

"But this isn't some sort of insurance or divorce thing you're working on?"

"No," I said, "definitely not."

For a minute, her brows puckered. The Angie I knew in the past was sharp as they came, and I got a sick feeling in my stomach she may be putting things together. Then the furrow eased, and she picked up her beer and drained it.

"Guess I'll just have to trust you."

"Does Marlow have a type?" I asked.

"Of woman, you mean?"

"Uh huh."

"From what I hear, I guess you could say he has a general type."

"How general?" I asked.

Angie grinned. "Over eighteen, under thirty, and not his wife."

I worked at keeping my poker face and hoped I was better at concealing things than Angie was at putting them together.

"Any indication he goes beyond the straight and narrow?" I asked.

"You have anything particular in mind?" she asked.

I took a deep breath, judging just how far I could go. "Off the record?"

"Yes, goddammit. Haven't we already gone over that? Just what are you wondering about?"

Despite trusting her, I took a minute to carefully go over things one more time. Although I needed answers, at the same time I had to protect Santiago's investigation.

"Any indication he can get violent?"

Angie took a moment to use her hand to smooth out some non-existent wrinkles in her left slack leg. Once she'd given herself enough time to pick her words, she looked back up at me.

"You're definitely not working on anything on the civil law end of things."

"Nope."

"You know, when you really think about it, despite our population, Providence is more like a small town than a city."

"True."

"Means it's awful hard to keep anything secret around here."

"Obviously."

She shook her head, her lips pursed. A stray lock of hair fell across her forehead, and she brushed it back without thinking. "I've honestly never heard anything like that."

"Is it possible?"

"I guess it's not impossible," she said, "but one thing you've got to realize is Marlow's been extremely careful when it comes to dipping his wick."

Breathing deep, I felt like doing something with my hands but couldn't think of anything that wouldn't feel awkward. I left them hanging at my sides.

"Careful how?"

The furrowing of the eyebrows again, and this time she pursed her lips as well. "One way of being careful would be to make sure you indulged your—predilections—somewhere else. If you had them, that is."

"Ah hah. Like up the road?"

"I mean like the other side of the state line, pick any direction you want."

Made sense in a way. With Providence smack dab in the middle of the state, two hours in any direction could you get across state lines.

"Would that be far enough? He'd still be a fairly prominent man. Surely, there'd be people who would recognize his name."

"You think so?" Angie asked.

"Of course."

"Then tell me, smart guy, what's the name of the mayor of, oh, let's say Springfield?"

"Uhm—"

"Or how about Jefferson City? It's right down the road, after all."

I frowned. "Okay. You made your point."

"Dammit, Quinton. What the hell are you into?"

"We made a deal, Angie."

She exhaled in frustration. "Fine. Since I'm already in for a penny . . ."

"Yeah?"

"I can't give you much more than I already have. Just whispers, and that's about it."

"It's alright. It was a long shot anyway."

"Goddammit, Quinton. Shut up and listen to me."

I leaned forward.

"I can't give you much more," she repeated, "except for the names of a couple of people I know who would probably be more than willing to talk to you."

CHAPTER NINETEEN

JUST LIKE THE DAY BEFORE, SANTIAGO AND I spoke the next morning before I'd gotten out the door.

"Anything?" he asked.

"A little movement," I said. "Nothing really specific to report."

"Dammit, Quinton. I thought I was hiring a professional."

"You did, Lieutenant. But if you change your mind and want me to back off, then go ahead and give the DNA findings to your detectives and see what happens."

There was about a thirty second silence, before the frazzled cop spoke again. "Sorry," he said. "The ticking clock is really weighing on me. Any day now, hell any hour, Krenshaw and Reynolds are going to come around looking for the results. Can you imagine what they'll think if they call down to the lab and find out I already received it?"

"I understand," I said, "and I'm doing what I can, but it takes time. Speaking of those two, did you know they braced me yesterday?"

"No, I didn't. Where, when and why?"

I gave him a quick rundown of my encounter with his two cops. After I finished, there was another, longer silence before the lieutenant spoke again. "They know you're involved somehow. That's not good."

"No, it's not," I said. "But it does lead to the question of why they've been having the girl's house monitored."

"Could just be this thing we call due diligence," Santiago said.

"Could be," I said. "Either way, it may be something to look into. Right now, I'm heading out to hopefully put another piece of the puzzle into place."

"You need anything from my end?" Santiago asked.

"Not that I can think of. Even if something comes up, we should hold it as a last resort, don't you think?"

Santiago didn't answer at first, and for some reason I visualized him holding his breath.

"Don't take this the wrong way, Quinton. But I really hate doing things this way, you know?"

"I understand," I said. "Any idea how much longer you can stall those two?"

"I'd say another day or two at most. If nothing else, one way or another things are going to start leaking out. You've got to find something for me."

"Hang in there, Lieutenant. Hopefully, I can find what you need, then just fade into the background and let the professionals take over."

"Let's hope to hell," the cop said before hanging up.

CHAPTER TWENTY

ADRIAN RIVERS HAD AN OFFICE on the second floor of the Providence City Building. Although being situated on the second floor of a five-story building would ordinarily indicate someone of low status, such wasn't the case with Rivers. If you'd stopped a hundred random people on the street and asked them who Adrian Rivers was, you'd maybe, if you were lucky, get one person who could tell you.

However, if you asked the same question of anyone who worked for the city, or Carson County for that matter, or who had any kind of commercial business with the Providence government, they'd for damn sure be able to identify Rivers.

The treasurer for the city of Providence, Rivers had been in his job for some time, at least a couple of decades. In his youth, he'd held a couple of lower-level city jobs while he worked his way through night school to become a CPA. Certificate in hand, he'd applied for the position in the treasury office about a year later and had been there ever since.

I've lived in the area for years now since returning from St. Louis, and the only reason I knew of Adrian Rivers was because of hearing the name bandied about now and then by off-duty cops or city workers working out at The Blaster. But I'd never met the man, and as I opened the door to the outer office of the Providence city treasurer, I wasn't sure what to expect.

Although I knew for sure what awaited me wasn't the dude in question.

"Can I help you?" asked an absolutely stunning young woman of some Asian ancestry. She sat behind a receptionist's desk, the only article of furniture in sight except for four padded, black leather chairs against one wall.

A few oil paintings spotted the walls here and there, most of them showing scenes out of nineteenth century California: missions, pueblos, and lone Indians riding in the desert. The pale blue color of the walls highlighted the artwork, making the images stand out.

All in all, it didn't impress me as a normal city government office. I felt more as if I'd stepped into a doctor or lawyer's office, or maybe that of an exclusive financial planner.

I guess when you've been in the same office for as many years as Adrian Rivers, you get to make a few concessions.

The furnishings didn't stand out as much as the woman behind the desk. Sitting down, I figured her at around five two or so. Long, glistening black hair swopped and swirled around her shoulders, offsetting a midnight blue dress of some sort of shimmery material. The tight fit of the dress showed that, at least from the waist up, the lady wasn't lacking for anything.

Without saying anything, I walked up and gave her one of my business cards. She read it, quirked her eyes at me, and started to hand it back.

I shook my head. "Please send it in to your boss," I said, "and ask him to read the back."

Instinctively, she began to flip the card over, then stopped herself and looked back at me.

"Whatever this is, sir, I'm not too sure it's appropriate."

"Maybe not," I said. "On the other hand, how much time and effort will it take to walk across this nice room, go in the man's office and give it to him. Fifteen seconds, tops?"

"Maybe he's busy," she said.

"Possibly. Or possibly he'd really like to talk to me if he knew I was out here. What do you say?"

She slid her fingers along the edges of the card for a second or two, then stood up. "Would you take a seat?" she asked. Without looking to see if I did, she headed off towards a far door I assumed led into her boss's office.

Half a minute later, she came back out and sat down behind her desk without looking at me. I wasn't sure what to think, so I took what seemed the only reasonable course of action.

I sat and waited.

I sat quietly for going on fifteen minutes before a slight buzz came from somewhere under the young woman's desk. She picked up a small ear bud, placed it in her ear, mumbled something too soft for me to catch, then took the bud out.

"He'll see you now," she said, gesturing down the hall to the inner office.

I stood up, smiled at her, and headed down the hall.

When I got to the door, it was closed. I knocked, and a distant voice said, "Come in."

Adrian Rivers was sitting behind a plain wooden desk, not much larger than an elementary teacher's desk. The rest of the room was done in as stark a manner: white walls, black shelves holding a variety of four-inch binders of multiple colors, and bare wood floors.

From what I understood, Rivers wasn't a native Midwesterner. He hailed from somewhere in California, thus explaining the art- work in the outer area, even though he'd lived here for most of his life. His tanned skin, dark eyes and dark hair laced through with silver betrayed his Hispanic heritage. Even sitting behind his desk, I could tell he was a slight man, and the steel-framed glasses he wore made him look like a bookkeeper.

He held my business card, revolving it back and forth in his hands.

Without a word, he gestured me towards one of the three chairs in front of his desk. They were exact matches for the padded chairs out in the reception area.

We stared at each other for a moment as Rivers tapped my card on his desk.

"You're Mr. Quinton?" he asked, in what felt like a stall for time.

"I am."

"And this is your card?" He began tapping it on the desk a little more emphatically.

"It is."

Rivers turned the card so that he could look at the back. "And you wrote this message on it?"

"I did."

What I'd written on the back of the card read "Let's Talk About Melissa."

He placed the card on the desk, shoved it a couple of inches to the side, and finally looked directly at me. "Do you know my daughter?"

"No, Mr. Rivers. I don't."

"Then what is there to talk about?"

"I don't know your daughter, but I do know a little about her. I know a few years back she was dating someone, and it could have ended better. She moved away, somewhere back east, afterwards."

Rivers nodded, though his face stayed impassive. The dude would make one hell of a poker player. "It was actually more like eight years ago," he said. "She's married now, and we have two grandchildren."

"That's nice," I said.

"Then why don't we get to the purpose of your visit? Your card says you're a private detective. Are you soliciting your services, or already working for someone?"

"Meaning am I here to extort you in some way?"

Rivers tipped his head, his expression staying the same. "It's an obvious question, isn't it?"

"It is," I said, beginning to feel like a ghoul for intruding into a stranger's family life, "but that's not why I'm here."

"For what then?"

"I'm here for information."

"About my daughter?" His voice had risen a bit, and a flinty sharpness flickered in his eyes.

For such a normal, bookkeeper-looking guy, I had the intense feeling I wouldn't want to cross over to his bad side.

"No, Mr. Rivers," I said. "I'm here for information about her former lover."

CHAPTER TWENTY-ONE

"Since you're here asking about him, I assume you already know who Melissa was involved with," Rivers said.

"Let's say I've got a hunch."

Rivers's lips quirked. "Okay, call it a hunch. Care to spell it out?"

"I think for a while, some years back, your daughter was involved with Robert Marlow."

"And, assuming for a moment that's even true, you're not here looking for some sort of payout or anything like that?"

"No, sir," I said, "information only."

Rivers leaned back and steepled his fingers under his chin. "I kept you waiting outside for a while."

I didn't get the feeling he wanted some sort of comeback, so I stayed silent.

"During that time," he continued, "I made a few phone calls."

"Not a bad way to spend the taxpayers' time," I said.

The lips quirked again. "I called several people I know in the police department."

"I would guess with your position as city treasurer you probably know most of the cops, to one degree or another," I said.

Now, besides the quirk his eyes lightened a bit. "Fair point. Let's say I called a couple of people in the department I know and trust."

"You speak to Ricky, the night-time janitor?" I asked. "He's about the most trustworthy guy there."

Rivers took his glasses off and rubbed the bridge of his nose. An odd gesture for so early in the day. Maybe the guy worked extra-long hours.

"Among other things, the people I spoke to mentioned your somewhat—flippant—attitude."

"Mr. Rivers, I'd probably agree with you if I knew what the hell flippant means. Can we just get down to what you want to say so we can get on with business?"

Rivers folded the glasses and placed them on the desk in front of himself. "Those I spoke with assured me that, while you may be a questionable businessman, you're essentially honest and can be trusted."

"I tend to agree," I said, "except for the questionable business-man part."

Rivers leaned back and placed his arms squarely on the arms of his chair. "Regardless, that being said, what is it you want to know? And please don't be offended if at any point I tell you to get the hell out."

"Fair enough. And I can assure you this remains confidential. Please understand I'm not looking to smear your family. In fact, it would be best for me if this conversation never gets repeated to anyone."

"I can assure you, Mr. Quinton. If things are going to go in the direction I expect, the last thing I'll want to do is blab it around. If you're thinking for even one minute of going after my daughter in any way—"

In that instant, the plain-looking bureaucrat faded away, and I saw potential danger in the man's eyes.

"Either way," Rivers continued, "it seems that at the moment I don't have a lot of options. Please proceed."

"Your daughter was involved with Mayor Marlow at some point, correct?"

"That would be correct. Though I have absolutely no clue how you found out."

"Doesn't matter," I said.

"It might matter to me."

"Remember what your cop buddies said. I can assure you it won't go beyond either myself or my source."

"I guess for now I have to accept that. Since you already know about Melissa's—dalliance—with the mayor, what are you here for?"

"Do you know how long they saw each other?" I asked.

Rivers frowned for a moment. "Once my wife and I found out what was going on, you can imagine Melissa was reluctant to talk to us about it. I couldn't tell you for sure. I got the impression that it was only for a short while, a month or so. My wife may have a clearer idea."

"Doesn't matter," I said. "No reason to bother her with this. Do you know how the two of them met?"

He frowned again, this time seemingly more at himself than me. "That I can tell you for sure, unfortunately. One summer, when she was a year from graduating college, Mel got an internship at a local accounting firm, the same accountants Marlow uses for his personal accounts. I'm pretty sure that's where they met up."

I thought for a second about Angie Tickman's comments about Marlow keeping his activities non-local. Maybe in terms of where he took his conquests, but there was a pattern developing of him preying on local women.

Now came the moment I'd been dreading. It wasn't so much because I was scared of Rivers's position in the local government. Truth be told, there wasn't all that much a guy like him could legally do to me.

No, it was more simply that I would hate to ask any father what I had to. In the end, though I could see no way around it.

"Mr. Rivers, did Marlow, to the best of your knowledge, ever hurt Melissa?"

His face tightened up, and he took in a quick sip of breath. Those clasped fingers of his gripped even harder while a flinty look appeared in his eyes.

"Why do you ask?"

"I can't really say," I said.

"You come in and ask me something like that, yet won't reveal why you want to know?"

"I'm conducting an investigation, obviously. If I gave you any information at all, it could lead to my client, who wants to remain anonymous."

He nodded, though his mouth puckered, and leaned back in his chair again. He spent a few minutes staring at the ceiling before looking back to me.

"I assume you mean hurt beyond a grown man taking advantage of a much-younger woman? If Marlow had done something like that, and I knew about it, don't you think I would have pressed charges?"

"He's the mayor," I said. "Has a lot of clout in town."

"And I'm the city treasurer. I have a fair degree of influence myself."

I nodded. "Then again, maybe it wouldn't have done any good to press charges."

"Why not?" Rivers asked.

"A whole lot of reasons. Maybe it would have made your daughter look bad. Maybe there wasn't any real evidence you could present. Or maybe . . ." I paused, the breath catching in my throat.

"Yes?" Rivers said.

"Or maybe you thought you could get something out of it," I said.

He closed his eyes for a moment, and I wondered just what he saw wherever he was looking.

I waited.

Finally, Rivers opened his eyes again. "Hole in one," he whispered. "Though not quite in the way you may be thinking."

I nodded in my best encouraging manner.

"You have to understand, I know very little of this directly. Most of Mel's side of the story I got from my wife, who got it from her. Easier thing for a girl to talk to her mother about this sort of thing than her father."

"I can see that."

Rivers paused, pinched the bridge of his nose again. "If you're asking did Bob Marlow ever attack Mel in any way, as far as I know the answer is no. Did he prey on a young girl in order to—satisfy himself? Absolutely. Did he treat her as pretty much a disposable toy for his own use? Without a doubt. Did he wreck the hell out of her self-esteem for a while there? Without question."

I took a breath and gave Rivers a moment to compose himself. For the last few seconds there, it had seemed as if he was trying to convince himself instead of me.

"So what you're saying," I eventually spoke up, "is the guy was pretty much of a tool but not much else."

Rivers stared at me without speaking, his eyes nearly snapping with some emotion I didn't even want to try to guess.

"One more thing," I said, "then I'll be out of your hair. Why didn't you ever go after Marlow in any way? Sure, your daughter was of age, still . . ."

"Bob's been our mayor for almost eight years," Rivers said.

"And you've been city treasurer for a couple of decades," I pointed out.

"Not nearly as glamorous a position, though. And one that doesn't exactly groom one for higher office. Even if it does allow me to hold a lot more sway than most people would think."

Even with my distaste for the man growing, I needed to keep my focus on the immediate objective. "Never hurts to have the mayor owing you a favor, does it?"

"No, it doesn't. Especially if they develop higher aspirations."

"Such as governor," I said.

Rivers smiled. "Such as governor."

"Even so, I'll bet you know where a lot of bodies are buried."

"I do indeed," Rivers said.

I clenched and unclenched my hands a couple of times. "You still could have screwed up his plans."

Rivers nodded, and now I got the idea he was only half looking at me. "At the very least I would have caused a ruckus."

I stopped clenching and took a deep breath. "You make some kind of deal with him?"

"I did indeed," Rivers said. "You may think it incredibly crass, a man treats your child like something disposable, never mind the age difference, and you decide to do business with him, but since nothing would have happened to him anyway, I figured to get something out of it."

"How old's Melissa?" I asked.

"Now? She's twenty-seven."

"And this happened when?"

Rivers paused and fixed me with a stern look. "Anything from this point on," he said, "I'll completely deny if you ever mention. Furthermore, as city treasurer, I have quite a few friends both locally and across the state. You make any of this public, and you may find it a lot harder when it comes time to renew your investigator's license."

I took a deep breath. I don't like being threatened, whether physically or financially, and for a moment I was tempted to stand up, tell Rivers what to do with himself, and leave. But I had the feeling I was about to find a few pieces of the puzzle for my client, and at the moment time was running out.

"Let's consider it like the news people do, deep background. Means I can use it, but not even indicate any names or details at all. How's that sound?"

Rivers frowned for a moment, then nodded. "I can live with that."

"Goes both ways, though, Mr. Rivers."

"Excuse me?"

"When I walk out of this office, you don't call, text, or shout from the rooftop anything about this. I don't want His Honor to have any idea I'm inquiring about him."

"I'm afraid you underestimate our good mayor," Rivers said. "While Marlow's not exactly the sharpest knife in the drawer, you really think his people don't have a handle on this town? If you've been at this more than a day, I'd say there's a good chance somebody already has some inkling."

I thought for a minute of James Ericson, the out-of-town PI, and wondered just how high any possible "handlers" went.

"Even so, no use helping them run me down."

"True enough," Rivers said. He leaned back in his chair and once again steepled his fingers together. "It's not a very pretty story, and don't think I haven't had my share of self-loathing over the years. I guess this is what a lifetime working in government brings you to."

"I wouldn't know about that," I said, "but I'd still like to hear the story."

"Okay then," Rivers replied. "Sit back and I'll fill you in."

CHAPTER TWENTY-TWO

I SPENT ABOUT AN HOUR DRIVING AROUND TOWN, no particular destination in mind, letting my brain absorb it all. My little visit with Adrian Rivers had left me wanting to go home and shower. Instead, I pulled into the downtown location of a small local sub chain and had a large Italian with everything on it.

Thus fortified, I went back to my car, climbed in, and called Santiago

"Marlow has a history of violence with women," I said by way of opening. On the other end, I heard Santiago take in a sip of air.

"You sure?" the detective boss asked.

"Yep, but there's a hitch."

"Such as?"

"The person who told me this did so in complete confidence. There's no way they're going to come forward at all."

"Well, hell. Why'd you promise that?"

"Come on, Lieutenant. Don't tell me you guys don't cut deals like this all the time."

"Of course, we do. However, we're duly authorized authorities. If your source, whoever it is, won't come forward what good will they do us?"

"Simple. For one thing, it's another check on one side of the equation. Let's assume for a moment that His Honor did in fact kill Laura Mosby. At his age, what are the odds that she was his first? Or even his second for that matter? Maybe not of killings, but of basic assault?"

"You saying we could show a pattern of him roughing up women?" Santiago asked.

"If the truth is out there, and you know to look for it, how hard would it be to find? Isn't it generally known around city government what a clodhopper the guy is?"

"More or less."

"There you go."

"So why hasn't anyone ever heard of this before? Clodhopper doesn't automatically equal serial abuser."

"Maybe not," I said, "but it's something more than you had this time yesterday."

Something like a grumble came over the phone. "Okay, give me what you've got."

I assumed Santiago was in his office, and considering the nature of the call he surely had his door shut. Even so, in the background I could faintly hear the hustle, bustle, and rigmarole of the squad room.

"The girl in question," I said, "is from this area. However, Marlow took her up to Kirksville for their dates. Get a good eighty miles away, and most people wouldn't know who the man is."

"What happened during the—ahh—date in question?" Santiago asked.

"I can give you the long version later. Short story is that clodhopper got a little carried away one night, maybe a little sloppy with his drinking, and somewhere in the heat of passion began strangling the girl."

A long moment of silence passed over the air before Santiago finally murmured, "Goddamn."

"About my feeling," I said.

It took a few seconds before Santiago spoke again. "Doesn't definitely prove anything," he said.

"Of course not. And in this case, the young woman lived to walk away. Turns out she went far away. But it gives a bit of background to see how he could get carried away and something would go horribly wrong."

"You know I need more, Quinton. Abbie Krenshaw was in my office this morning bugging me to put some heat on the lab to get the DNA back. I managed to stall her off, but not for much longer. If I'm going to aim them in the mayor's direction, I've got to have more ammunition."

I wondered, not for the first time in the last few days, if Santiago's concern was really for the welfare of his people or himself. If Reynolds and Krenshaw moved against Marlow, there was no way it would not come down on their commander. Was I merely serving the out-of-towner's own selfish interest?

When it came down to it, I really didn't know a whole lot about what made Santiago tick.

"Okay," I said, "let's look at it this way. One, you have the DNA. Either way it plays, you know the mayor was in her bedroom, and even a first-year law student could make a case as to why."

"I don't know about first year," Santiago said. "Second year maybe."

"Two," I said, kind of surprised the lieutenant had a sense of humor. "Laura Mosby was strangled, and our good public official has at least some history of getting carried away with his bed partners."

"Okay."

"And three, if you know one and two, it shouldn't be all that hard to make a case he likes to fool around with younger women."

"Hell," Santiago said, "in a lot of circles that last one would just make him a regular guy."

I grinned. "It would, but we're not talking just any regular Joe Six-pack, are we?"

Santiago sighed, deeply, and for a moment there I could almost feel the weight on him. "No," he said, "we're not. We're talking a guy who's making noises about a run for governor."

"True," I said. "However, there's another side to this you may not have thought of."

"Oh really. Would that be the side that says that, if Marlow did it, for a criminal wannabe he's made a pretty good job of covering his tracks? That he's pulled off a so-far flawless murder which has us dumb cops running in circles? And that anyone who's spoken two sentences with the man wouldn't credit him with that much intelligence?"

"Well, yeah," I said. "That's about what I was thinking. Wouldn't your best guess be if he did kill the Mosby girl it was more of an accidental type thing?"

"That's how I'd read it," Santiago said.

"Which leads to a very interesting question."

"It does indeed," Santiago said. "If he was with Laura that night, and things got a little heated, he could easily have screwed up. If that's true . . ."

"Yeah," I said.

"Who's helping him cover it up?"

CHAPTER TWENTY-THREE

Talking with Santiago put me in a foul mood. I'd taken this job both as a favor to the lieutenant, though God knows why as he didn't exactly rank as my biggest fan on the force, and because there wasn't much else going on at the moment.

It had seemed a fairly simple task. Within a few days, see if there was any possible connection between a specific suspect and a specific crime. The only thing that made it somewhat special was the identity of the suspect in question.

Now, in just a few days, the damned thing had mushroomed into this complex affair involving the police suspecting me of some sort of shenanigans; a chunk of the city political structure potentially taking aim at me, if Adrian Rivers was any authority, and why wouldn't he be; and elements from out of town, in the person of James Ericson, private eye, running around my territory.

What had seemed an interesting little puzzle at first had become a complete cluster.

Added to this was the fact that, eventually, Detectives Reynolds and Krenshaw would get their hands on the information their boss was keeping hidden, and the whole damned thing would blow wide open.

Okay, then. Time for Plan B, which essentially was to forget it all for a while.

I went back to my place to detox. Did a few basic home repairs I'd been putting off, then grilled a couple of cheeseburgers, threw the works on them, and had them for dinner while I watched the beginning of what ended up being a dismal Royals game. After suffering through the game, I stayed on the couch and watched a few late-night reruns before hauling myself off to bed.

The next morning, I woke up somewhat refreshed, feeling more or less in one piece, and with a definite plan of action in mind.

Not sure if it was a good plan, or even a rational one, but it was a course of action.

First, I made a few phone calls.

The first was to Talia Sanderson. She and I had made plans get together, and I wanted to make sure we were still on.

Or maybe I just felt like hearing her voice.

She said sure, asked me how my week was going and if I could say anything more about the big case (I couldn't), then thanked me for delaying, even for a few minutes, her having to go into a faculty meeting. However, the torture couldn't be put off forever, and after a few more minutes of idle chatter, she had to disengage and head off.

I wasn't sure if my next call would be answered, even if the person were available, so my day began looking up when he picked up after the first ring.

"Yes?"

"It's me," I said.

"No kidding," James Ericson said. "What can I do for you?"

"Wondered if you were still in town," I said.

A pause, and I could almost see the gears turning in Ericson's head. "What if I am," he finally said. "There a law against that?"

"Not at all. I just thought maybe we could get together and compare notes."

He gave out a short, brief chuckle. "You mean you want to tap my head again? Maybe figure out about how I fit into this whole thing? Who my client is?"

I decided it wouldn't hurt to throw a shot in the dark. "Maybe I know who it is."

Ericson chuckled again, though this one sounded a bit forced. "I doubt that. I'd like to think I'm professional enough to keep my back covered."

"If you're not working for the girl's family, and she doesn't have any personal connections down your way, my guess is that finding out who murdered her isn't your top priority."

"Not bad, gym man. But if I'm not after her killer, who or what would I be after?"

A sudden thought came to mind, and I'd almost uttered it before my common sense clamped it down. "Damned if I know," I said as a feeble way to cover myself.

Ericson's chuckle now became a full-out laugh. "Uh huh. That's about what I thought. Nothing personal, Quinton, you sure you're any good at this detecting stuff?"

I figured my best move was to disengage before I made any more of a fool of myself.

Besides, last night, somewhere between the cheeseburgers, the sucky ball game, and the lame re-runs, a plan had come to mind.

Maybe not the best of plans, but one nonetheless.

Ericson was still a dead end as I'd pretty much expected.

Time to stop stalling, then, and kick things into gear.

CHAPTER TWENTY-FOUR

BEFORE HEADING OUT, I MADE MY THIRD and final call of the morning. After speaking with the person on the other end for a few minutes, I got a grudging agreement to give me some time.

A few minutes later, I was in the Cherokee and zipping to the downtown area.

"I didn't really expect to see you again," Adrian Rivers said once we had settled in his office.

"Like a bad penny, as my grandma used to say," I said. He was wearing a pink shirt with a navy-blue tie with red paisleys on it. I didn't know they still made men's ties with paisleys Then again my usual attire is jeans and a tee-shirt, sometimes a sweat shirt in the winter. Rivers had a fancy-looking pen in his hand that he twirled back and forth, sort of how he'd done my card the day before.

He was also wearing a frown, bordering on a grimace, directed straight at me.

"You say bad penny," Rivers said. "I'm thinking more a goddamned nuisance. What is it you want now? And I have a meeting with the city manager at ten, so whatever it is make it quick."

"Fair enough," I said, "but a little background first. My impression during our last sitdown was that, in regards to the mayor and your daughter, you were making the most of a bad situation."

"I as much as told you so myself. And if you're thinking of using anything I said publicly, I'm going to remind you that you gave your word you wouldn't."

His expression told me Rivers didn't think my word was worth all that much.

Maybe I should have worn a paisley tie.

"No problem," I said, "and I'm not going to reveal anything. That's not why I'm here."

Rivers stopped twirling the pen and gripped it tighter. "Then why are you here, Mr. Quinton? I thought we covered everything yesterday, so would you please just tell me what you want?"

"I'd like you to get ahold of Mayor Marlow. Give him a call, preferably today. Even though it may be hard to track down a politician on a Friday."

"And just why would I do that?" By the whiteness of his fingers, I was afraid Rivers was going to snap his pen in half.

"Because I've been hassling you. Coming to your office. Showing up in your neighborhood. I've been bugging you to tell me what went on between the mayor and your daughter in the past."

Rivers's eyebrows notched in confusion. "I've already told you . . ." he paused, and the notch smoothed out. "You want him to know about your investigation?"

I nodded and gave the man a beaming smile. "Right. You said yesterday there was a chance he's already aware of me. I want to remove any doubt."

Rivers put the pen down and placed his hands flat on his desk. "That could be dangerous," he said. "Don't be deceived by Bob's 'aw shucks' folksiness when he's being interviewed on TV. He may know one or two—ah—experienced people."

My thoughts exactly. Hopefully, people experienced enough to know how to clean up a crime scene to get rid of evidence.

"I'm counting on it," I told Rivers.

"And this will end our business?" he asked.

"It will."

"In that case," Rivers Said. "Consider it done. And good luck. I think you'll need it."

CHAPTER TWENTY-FIVE

LATE ON A FRIDAY MORNING, THE NEWSROOM of the *Providence Tribune* looked almost deserted. Out of a bank of around thirty desks, six were occupied, while three others had empty chairs but computer screens up and running. The desks at all the other chairs were empty with ten of those desks completely bare, not even a coffee cup on them.

Towards the back of the large room, about five steps away from a glass-enclosed office, I saw Angie Tickman hunched over her keyboard. No one looked up at my entrance as I made my way over to her.

"Second time in a week," Angie said as I plopped myself in an empty chair next to her desk. "Should I feel flattered?"

"Depends," I said as I looked around. "Is it always this empty around here?"

Angie grimaced. "Late morning, Quinton. Deadline was about ten hours ago, which means most of the straight news people are only now rearing themselves out of bed."

I glanced at the desks with no furnishings of any kind. "How many of those straight news people left these days?"

"Tell the truth, not that many. And those who are often are so young they don't know an adjective from a conjunction."

"Neither do I," I said, "which is why I leave that kind of stuff to you professionals."

"So what's up? You here for more information, or maybe ready to spill the beans on your big case?"

I grimaced and slumped my shoulders. "How about doing me a favor?"

"Thought I already did you one the other day."

"Yeah, but this one would be a little more fun."

Angie turned from me and looked around the newsroom. If anything, the activity in there had ebbed in the last few minutes. Two of the people who'd been at their desks had disappeared, and another was up and heading towards what I assumed was the coffee room.

Angie pointed towards the enclosed office in the corner.

"That belongs to Hal Timmins, the managing editor," she said.

"Looks a lot like Lieutenant Santiago's setup over at headquarters."

She shrugged. "Any more he spends most of his day in there, door closed. Handles almost all the grunt work through instant messaging."

"A boss for the twenty-first century."

Angie settled down in her chair. "I'm not all that old, Sam."

"I'm aware."

"Young enough, in fact, that even when I first started it was clear what the future held for newspaper work."

"Makes sense."

"And digital, while necessary to the bottom line, isn't quite as exciting as seeing your words actually printed out on paper."

"You're a romantic," I said. "Kind of a dying breed."

She wrinkled her nose at me. "Maybe. The point is, while I knew what I was getting into back then, things just aren't all that fun or exciting around here anymore."

"Maybe I can spice it up a bit."

Angie peered up at me. "And just how would you go about doing that?"

"Maybe I've been hassling you, imposing on our past relationship."

"So what else is new?"

"Asking you all sorts of questions about the mayor. Pressuring you to fess up to all kinds of nasty little rumors and such."

"Okay," Angie managed to drawl the word out till it filled half a dozen syllables. "And then what?"

"And then you've decided to hell with it, told me to take a leap, and decided to pass word of all my questions on to someone who has the mayor's ear."

It took several seconds for Angie to reply. "Uhm, Sam, this is starting to cross a line."

"What line?" I asked.

"Sounds like you're asking me to become a part of the story. That's kind of against Journalism 101."

"Not the way I see it. Are you doing a story of any kind on the mayor?"

"You mean, at this moment? No."

"Isn't what I just laid out exactly what I was asking you about the other day?"

She mulled that one over a moment before answering. "Maybe a bit exaggerated, but other than that no."

"Then, if by chance you have the ear of someone who has the ear of someone who has the mayor's ear, you're just going to be passing along the truth about something that doesn't directly bear on your work."

"I hear the sound of several hairs being split," Angie said. "Let me get this straight. You're wanting me to sic Marlow and his friends on you?"

"You wouldn't be the only one," I said.

"You mean you're planting these seeds around with other people?"

"Something like that."

Now she sat up straight, and flames began smoldering in her eyes. "What the hell, Quinton? Do you have any idea just what you're getting into? Exactly how bad is this thing, whatever it is?"

"Trust me, Angie. Reporter or no, you don't want to know yet. And like I said the other night, if it's nothing, no one will get hurt, including me. If it's something, you'll have a front row seat for one hell of a story."

"One I may not get to write if it gets out I was involved in any way."

"Who's going to tell?" I asked.

She smoldered at me for a few more moments, then relaxed back in her seat, almost as if her cord had been cut.

"What the hell," she said, "it's not like there's been anything exciting going on lately. Any chance there's going to be a gunfight outside City Hall?"

When I didn't answer directly, Angie peered closer. "Quinton?"

"You never know," I said.

CHAPTER TWENTY-SIX

Talia Sanderson showed up at my place at 6:30 on the dot. One thing I could never fault her for, among several, was her punctuality. Probably came from scheduling and juggling all the meetings she had all day long.

As soon as she walked in the door, she sniffed and smiled. "BBQ?"

"Yep."

Her face fell. "Cooked by you?"

"Nope."

Her face rose again.

"Lou's?" At her mention of the new, slightly-expensive restaurant that had just settled into the downtown area I nodded, and she gave a full-on beam as she handed me a six-pack of Heineken.

"For you, then."

Nodding my appreciation, I reached out to give her a big hug and ran my hand up and down her spine. She was wearing a maroon, sleeveless cotton top with the top two buttons undone, white slacks and sandals. Her hair smelled freshly washed.

"I'm guessing this isn't your casual Friday work outfit?" I said as I headed into the kitchen.

Talia walked over and sat on one end of my couch. "As per orders from the college chancellor, casual Friday's for faculty and staff, not for administrators."

I poured a glass of her favorite wine and walked into the living room with it. "Considering how they ordinarily dress, how can you tell when your faculty's doing casual Friday?"

She took the wine, wrinkled her nose at me in appreciation. "Their blue jeans have more than the usual number of holes in them. You're kind of spiffed up yourself."

I was indeed. At least, spiffed up by my standards: fresh khakis, dark blue button up shirt (short-sleeved, of course, besides it being summertime, got to show the guns every chance you get), and I'd even shaved for the occasion.

My phone buzzed. I went over to the kitchen counter where it sat, looked at the incoming message, and picked it up.

"Yeah?"

"They got the report," Santiago said as a greeting.

"How'd that happen?" I asked.

"Krenshaw finally got either fed up or suspicious, one or the other, and called up the lab on her own. I'm glad I wasn't standing right there when she found out I've had it for a week. As it was, storming into my office an hour later, she almost scorched me where I sat."

"Good thing you're a tough Chicago cop," I said.

"Tough Chicago's got nothing to do with it. If Matt Reynolds and your buddy Josh Nichols hadn't been there to hold her back, she probably would have gouged my eyes out."

"Doesn't attacking a superior officer rank as some sort of insubordination charge?" I asked. From her perch on the couch, Talia gave me a speculative look. I winked at her.

"Probably would," Santiago said, "if I didn't pretty much agree with her. Actually, I kind of admire her restraint. If one of my bosses had ever pulled a stunt like this on one of my cases, I probably would have yanked out my piece and shot them in the shoulder."

I walked into the kitchen, pulled down the over door, and checked on my simmering arrangement of brisket, twice-baked potatoes and summer sausage.

"So what now?" I asked the boss cop.

"Now I yank your chain. Thanks for helping in this, but I had no choice except to lay it out for them. Mayor Marlow is now officially a suspect in the murder of Laura Mosby."

"Probably just as well it's out in the open," I said, "but I've got a little problem."

"Don't see how. Tote up what you're owed, send it on to me, and depending on how this shakes out I'll either send you a voucher some day or pay you out of pocket."

Talia was shooting me an inquisitive look, probably the same look she gave students when they came in her office complaining their professors wouldn't grade on a curve, and I held up a finger in a "just a moment" motion.

"Actually," I said, "there's two problems. Have you forgotten James Ericson snooping around this?"

"The PI from Rolla? No, hadn't forgotten. Just don't really care. If he crosses our paths officially, we'll deal with it then. Don't see how it's your concern. What's the other problem?"

I told Santiago about the trails of bread crumbs I'd started leaving around town. When I finished, I was met with silence on his end and the mother of all glares from Talia.

Took about three heartbeats for the lieutenant to come back to earth. "What the fuck were you thinking, Quinton?"

"I was thinking that you needed some kind of indicator about how dirty the mayor is. If he isn't, when word gets back to him he'll either ignore it, protest in some mild way, or at the worst threaten a slander suit. However, if he's guilty . . ."

"Then he'll do something worse," Santiago finished.

"Right. And if it's door number two, then you'd have your confirmation, or at least a pointer in the right direction."

"Except all that's unnecessary now because Reynolds and Krenshaw have the report."

"How soon they going to act on it?" I asked.

"Not right away. They're planning on doing about forty-eight hours of surveillance before deciding whether or not to bring him in for questioning. God, even saying it makes my stomach clench."

"Then there's a little time yet," I said.

"Time for what?"

"To see if I catch anything with the bait I set out."

Talia frowned even harder as a slight hiss came over the phone. "Didn't you hear me a minute ago, Quinton? You're out of it. Now that my people know the score . . ."

"Doesn't change anything in terms of here and now. I've already put out the feelers, and even if you say I'm out of it, Marlow and his people may well have me in their sights. If you know a way of calling them off, I'm all for it."

A bit of grumbling now. At least better than a hiss. "I hope you know what you're doing," Santiago said. "Take care, and let me know if anything comes up."

"Will do, Lieutenant. Now, if you don't mind, I've got a fetching young lady sitting on my couch who's beginning to look a little put out."

The cop clicked off without another word, and I turned my full attention to Talia.

"Fetching?" she said, one eyebrow cocked at me. "Just how ancient are you, mister?"

I grinned. "If I'd said gorgeous or ravishing, Santiago wouldn't have believed me. How's about dinner?"

"Before that, did I hear you right? It almost sounded like you've made yourself a target for someone."

I went back into the kitchen, pulled our meal out of the oven, and carried it into the dining room. As we sat down, Talia gave me a look.

"Well?" she finally said.

"Sorry, but it's work. Can't get into it without breaking all kinds of rules."

"Have to keep things confidential?" she asked.

"Unfortunately, yeah."

"I don't like it."

"I know," I said. "Sometimes, neither do I."

CHAPTER TWENTY-SEVEN

After a quiet weekend, the first salvo came at seven thirty on Monday morning as I was buffing and polishing some of the equipment in the gym. Lisa Nolan was taking a rare day off work, and Keri Eckland, her assistant, hadn't yet shown up. We open at seven on the weekdays, and there were only two clients on the premises, forty-something brunettes in matching pink and yellow spandex spotting each other on one of the pull-down machines.

Considering I was planning on spending most of the day cleaning, I was wearing faded khaki shorts, an old Midwest Wrestling League tee-shirt, and a black headband. Dressing that morning, I'd considered wearing one of my old Blonde Bomber shirts, maybe the one with me glaring through slitted eyes while extending a clenched fist, but figured it would come off a little too much like bragging.

I was crouched down on both knees, scrubbing pad in one hand and bottle of metal cleaner in the other, when the front door opened. A wisp of hot summer air, even early morning it was in the low eighties, alerted me, and I looked up to see a man standing in the doorway, his phone in hand.

He stood average height, five eight or so. It was hard to tell his weight for sure because he wore a baggy, cotton jacket similar to what Don Johnson used to wear on *Miami Vice*. Judging by the pudginess of his face, he probably could have lost ten pounds or so.

He had short brown hair, almost military cut, though not quite so severe. While he probably thought the expensive, loosely-cut jacket made him look stylish, he actually came off as a little boy playing dress up in his father's clothes.

The man looked down at his phone again, glanced my way, gave a slight nod and put the phone away. He then began walking in my direction, both hands in his coat pockets.

I stood up while keeping my knees slightly bent. Without turning my head, I checked out the two women clients working their lats. As far as I could tell, they were totally engrossed in their workout.

The man kept coming my way.

I wanted to glance longingly to my office, where I had a gun in a desk drawer, but didn't really see the point.

Some months back, I'd been involved in a case that had, in a kind of sideways angle, concerned the local mob boys. As far as I knew, I'd ended things on good terms with the local head man, and last I'd heard he was still in charge, sort of, and running things in the Providence area.

Still, one never knew with those people. Could be that, for whatever reason, the local boss had decided to tie up a loose end. Or maybe someone above him had made the decision.

A more likely possibility, of course, was Bob Marlow had gotten my message and was a lot more connected than I'd given him credit for. Either way, I was plotting my best moves considering the only weapons I had were a greasy rag and a bottle of metal cleanser. The biggest concern was that, if worse came to worst, could I somehow save myself and protect the two women at the same time.

The man stopped four feet in front of me, hands still in pockets, and I could see he wore brown, wire-rimmed glasses.

Maybe my first hunch had been wrong. The dude looked about as far from a syndicate hit man as you could get.

Then again, could have just been protective coloration, so to speak.

"Mr. Quinton?" he said, his voice about half an octave above normal range for a man, and I relaxed a tad.

In the movies and TV, the hired killer always asks the victim to identify themselves, to make sure they have the right mark. Since the guy had been looking at his phone, I assumed he had a picture of me. If so, he'd have no need to revert to the cliché of calling out his victim's name.

"That's me," I said, still keeping a slight crouch and my muscles half tensed.

"My name is Stan Raimes," the man said.

"What can I do for you?"

"Hopefully quite a lot." He glanced over to where the two ladies were taking a break, sitting on each side of the machine and patting themselves down with towels. One was drinking from a plastic water bottle, and while I couldn't make out the brand name, I guessed it was the type of water where the price of one bottle would about equal my monthly utility bill.

"Could we talk somewhere in private?" Stan Raimes asked.

I still wasn't entirely at ease. "Right here's fine for me."

He looked again at the two women clients, then pitched his voice a little lower. "I work for the city, Mr. Quinton. In fact, I'm the mayor's chief of staff, and I really don't think you want to have this conversation in public."

I smiled at Raimes, capped the bottle of cleanser, and motioned with my arm to the back of the gym. "Right this way."

CHAPTER TWENTY-EIGHT

W HEN WE ENTERED MY OFFICE, I sat down behind my desk
and motioned Raimes to one of the client seats. He stood
for a moment, looking around, before sitting down.

May have been my imagination, but I thought I saw a slight
sneer on his face.

"So what can I do for you?" I asked.

"I'm here on behalf of Robert Marlow."

"Providence's esteemed mayor," I said.

Raimes cocked an eye at me. "Sarcasm, Mr. Quinton?"

"Not at all. Just wanted to make sure we were talking about
the same Bob Marlow. There must be a couple of others lurking
around somewhere."

A tinge of frostiness came over his tone. "You may remember
that I introduced myself as a member of the mayor's staff not two
minutes ago."

"As I recall, you introduced yourself as his chief of staff."

"Correct."

"Is that a for real title?" I asked.

"Excuse me?"

"Well," I said, slouching down a bit. "Presidents have chiefs of
staff, and I'm pretty sure governors do as well. Maybe even mayors
in places like New York or LA. But in Providence, MO? Is that an
actual title, or just something you like to tell yourself?"

Raimes's eyes smoldered, and I had even more the idea of a

little boy playing dress up. While I had the urge to keep pushing his buttons, going too far would probably be counterproductive.

"You've been asking questions about the mayor," he said, his cheeks clenched and clearly working to keep his voice level. "I want to know why."

"You want to know?" I asked.

"Let's say the mayor wants to know. What exactly is your interest in him?"

"Maybe I'm just a concerned citizen wanting to ensure local government works to its fullest."

A long moment passed between us before Raimes spoke up again. "Or maybe you're just a two-bit bottom feeder who's looking to make a cheap buck somehow."

I waved an arm, which took in all of my office, including the two client chairs, one filing cabinet, second-hand coffeemaker on mini fridge in the corner, and up on the wall my championship belt from the Midwest Wrestling League which, I'd noticed the other day, was starting to tarnish around the edges.

Most people focus on the Belt right off. The fact that Raimes didn't could mean he wasn't a wrestling fan. Or he didn't care for sports at all.

Then again, it could mean he simply hadn't noticed it.

Maybe I should get to polishing it instead of working on the equipment out front.

"All this looks two-bit to you?" I asked.

Raimes stood up, his right hand moving to brush some of his hair back into place. "You will cease and desist in your inquiries about the mayor," he said. "You will do so, or you will suffer severe consequences."

He turned, the shoulders of his sport jacket bunching a bit, and headed toward the door. I waited until his hand was on the knob before speaking.

"Don't think so."

Raimes paused, even through the loose jacket his shoulders and neck tensing up. He turned back to me.

"Excuse me?"

"If His Honor wants me to be intimidated, he needs to send someone with a little more heft. I'm not saying I've been investigating the mayor, though if I have, I think I'm going to keep on doing so. Clear?"

"Very clear, Mr. Quinton. And just between you and me, if I were you I'd be expecting someone with more 'heft' as you call it to come along fairly soon."

With that, mustering as much dignity as he could, Raimes walked out of my office.

At least he didn't do something childish like slam the door behind him.

Someone with more heft, huh?

"I'm counting on it," I said to the empty room.

CHAPTER TWENTY-NINE

T HE SECOND SALVO, OTHERWISE KNOWN AS more heft, showed up that night.

Talia and I had just squirreled into a booth in Gino's, a divey-looking place with probably the best pizza in town. I had upscaled, slightly, from the gym shorts and tee-shirt of earlier in the day and now wore a clean pair of jeans and, in a nod to the fact some serious summer temps were beginning to creep into the area, tan tee-shirt and light cotton blazer.

For the life of me, I couldn't tell if Talia had gone home to change after leaving work or not. There was so little difference between her professional attire at the university and what she wore for relaxation. This night, for instance, she had on dark green slacks, a cream-colored silk blouse, and plain gold earrings.

"Did you come straight here from work?" I asked.

Talia crinkled her nose at me. "Why do you ask?"

"Because if you dress like that at the university, I'm surprised any of your male faculty can keep their eyes off you."

Another crinkle. I was on a roll tonight.

"You're forgetting that it's almost mid-June, which means most of our faculty, at least the senior ones, are long gone for the summer."

I took a drink of water from a glass that had been set down for me right before Talia showed up. "Far as that goes, why do administrators have to work in the summer if faculty don't?"

Another crinkle. "Probably because we don't have a union and they do."

We fell to skimming over the menus to figure out what we wanted on our pizza when two uniformed officers showed up at our booth.

Talia and I looked up.

"Sam Quinton?" the older officer, around my age with dabs of gray mixing in his black hair, asked.

"Why so formal, Bill?" I asked. "You've worked out at my place enough to know who I am."

Bill Wallace grinned and jerked a thumb to the younger man next to him, a blond kid who still had a little bit of baby fat padding his jaw. "Reed here's a rookie, still by-the-book. Figured I'd make a good show for him."

Across from me, Talia was looking a little confused.

"Okay," I said, "so you put on your show. What's up?"

Bill Wallace glanced around. Gino's was filling up quickly. It's a little hole in the wall spot only the locals know, somehow having flown under the radar of the college students who flick in each year. Now, with the student population rapidly depleted, more grown-ups were showing up downtown, with Gino's being one of the main destinations.

Even so, it was still fairly early on a week night, leaving the closest occupied table about five feet away.

Wallace lowered his voice a little. "Guy outside wants to see you."

Knowing he must have had a good reason for speaking softly, I did the same. "What guy?"

"Better if you just come with us, Sam."

Something flickered in my memory, a little thing I'd heard in passing a few months back. It had been one afternoon when Wallace and a couple of his cop buddies were working out together. They were over at the free weights, what few Lisa Nolan's kept in the gym, and as I walked by had been discussing their newest assignments.

A momentary passing, the words absorbed but ignored right away.

Until now.

I turned to Talia. "I have to step outside for a minute, okay?"

By now, her face had turned a little pale. "Is everything . . ."

"It's fine," I said as I patted her hand. "Right, Bill? Everything's cool?"

"It's cool," Bill said. "Someone just wants to talk."

I brushed Talia's hand again. "Order whatever sounds good. I'll be back before the food gets here."

I walked with the two cops, past several diners trying to act like they weren't watching us, and outside of Gino's we headed around the corner to a waiting Cadillac. The guy sitting behind the driver's wheel looked to be about the size of the Sphinx. Bill Wallace gestured to me, and I opened up the rear door of the Caddy and crawled in.

As I'd figured, Mayor Bob Marlow was sitting in the back seat. We looked at each other for a moment before the mayor spoke.

"You don't seem all that surprised to see me," he said by way of introduction.

"Not really," I said. "Bill works out at my gym. A couple of months ago I heard something about how he had a new gig working on the mayor's detail. What's up?"

The mayor was a bit portly, as my grandmother used to say. He was of average height and somewhat overweight. Ordinarily, the extra pounds wouldn't have been a big deal, but for some reason, he carried them worse than most guys would. His was a soft fat, giving him something of a Pillsbury Doughboy appearance.

I wasn't exactly sure of his age, somewhere in the mid-fifties probably. His eyes were a watery brown, and his hair a rather limp salt and pepper. As we sat there scoping each other out, I tried to picture him riding the wave with a young woman like Laura Mosby.

Hard to imagine, unless she did most of the riding. Then again, it's amazing what a little prestige and importance can do for some guys.

Marlow shrugged and moved his hands in a kind of "what's up" gesture. They were as soft and pale as the rest of him, and I tried to imagine those hands strangling and killing a full-grown woman.

I couldn't quite see it.

Then again, it's sometimes amazing what people can do in the heat of the moment, passion or something else.

"You've been asking questions about me," Mayor Marlow said. "I'd like to know why."

"Didn't your boy Raimes tell you about our meeting this morning?"

"He did. He said you were somewhat uncooperative. Certain highly-placed people have told me that you're kind of raising a fuss. Again, I'd like to know why."

I only knew of one "highly-placed" person I'd spoken to, but I didn't know for sure how many ears Angie Tickman had managed to reach. Then again, as far as I knew Adrian Rivers could be a simple blabbermouth. Could be half the city hall knew by now I was investigating the mayor.

Regardless, Marlow sat there expectantly, and I had the feeling if I wanted to get out of the car without bruising my knuckles on his driver, I had to give him something.

"I'm guessing you know about my line of work," I said.

Marlow snorted. "You own a run-down flea trap health club and spend your spare time as a hired snooper. I wouldn't really call either of those work."

For a moment there, I toyed with a clear solution to Lt. Santiago's dilemma. All I had to do was let Lisa Nolan know what Marlow had said about The Blaster, and she'd probably run the mayor over with a semi-truck.

Problem solved.

Except it wouldn't really bring closure to Laura Mosby's family.

"I'm licensed by the state of Missouri to act as a private investigator," I said, considering the circumstances summoning as much dignity as possible. "And that's what I'm doing."

"Is it now?" Marlow said. "Are you investigating crimes, or something else?"

"Such as?"

The mayor snorted in exasperation and settled himself deeper into his seat. "I can come up with two guesses."

"Okay."

"One," he said as he raised up his hand to tick the points off with his fingers, "is that you're working for my soon-to-be third ex-wife, trying to give her enough ammo to go ahead and pull the trigger on the divorce she's always blabbing on about."

"Gun analogies aside," I said, "I'm not confirming or denying. What's the other possibility?"

The mayor's eyes hooded over, and an expression one could almost call crafty spread across his face. "Two," he did the finger tick thing again, "is close to number one. You're working to dig up whatever dirt you can on me."

"For someone other than your wife?" I asked.

The sly look, if anything, deepened. "I'm guessing you've heard about my, ah, political aspirations."

"You mean running for governor." As I said the words, I noticed something odd about Marlow. Most politicians like to preen and pump out their chest about seeking higher office. Some of them can't get through a five-minute conversation without falling into a "good of the people" speech.

When I mentioned the governorship, Marlow, if anything, seemed to deflate a little, and a kind of far-away look came into his eyes.

Whatever he was thinking or feeling, though, didn't come across in his words. "That's right," he said. "And it's not all that much of a stretch to imagine there's some people, even in my own party, who don't want me to run very far or very fast."

James Ericson from Rolla popped into my head.

"You think I'm a dirty tricks operator?" I asked.

He looked me over. After a moment, he shook his head. "No, I'm more inclined to think you're just a two-bit scuz who's looking for some sort of quick payday."

"Two-bit scuz isn't exactly the best way to refer to your taxpayers," I said.

"Maybe not. But I've dealt with bottom feeders like you most of my life. Like I said, I already got two ex-wives and working on a third. You think I don't know how people like you operate? So why don't you tell me who you're working for, and we can both go our way."

"Really?" I asked. "You're not going to have Bruno there drop me in a lake somewhere?"

Marlow's face reddened, though more in a frustrated than an angry way. "You don't get what you're up against, do you? Let me put it this way, Quinton. Whatever game you're playing, I can guarantee you you're out of your league. If you were smart, you'd tell me what I want to know, then walk away."

"Sorry," I said, "there's this thing called client confidentiality."

Marlow shook his head and leaned back in his seat, slightly squirming, as if he had an itch he couldn't reach. "May want to reconsider that position, sonny. There's people out there bigger than you. Hell, they're bigger'n me. If they take issue with you snooping around, don't say I didn't warn you."

"I'll consider myself warned," I said. "Can I go now?"

The mayor's face set a bit, as if he was considering saying something more. Then a slight smile came on his face. "Beat it, Quinton. For your own sake, I'm giving you one good warning. Whoever you're working for, whatever you're looking into, it's not worth your life. Trust me."

He motioned to the door. With one last glance at the driver, who hadn't so much as tensed his neck the whole time, I got out of the car. Bill Wallace and his partner stood there waiting on me, and as soon as I hit the sidewalk the Caddie slipped into gear and pulled away.

"His Honor manage to reason with you?" Wallace asked.

"About as much as anyone ever does," I said.

"That little, huh." Wallace shook his head and smiled. He glanced at his partner, then turned back to me. "Be careful around him, Sam. The mayor may look and act like a goofball, but he has clout to use when he wants to."

"That's part of my puzzle," I said.

"Huh?"

"I've got to figure out where his clout comes from."

I gave Wallace a nod, then turned and walked back into Gino's. As I sat back down at our table, Talia gave me a look.

"Well?" she asked after I didn't volunteer any information.

"Give me a minute, hon. I'm thinking something through."

As I'd told Wallace, where the mayor got his clout was a concern, but it wasn't the only one.

Granted, I'd only spent a couple of minutes talking with the man, but his in-person demeanor came off a lot different than little snippets you'd see of him on the news. Which led to my other confusion.

For the first time in this whole affair, no matter how I tried, I couldn't picture Marlow as a killer.

CHAPTER THIRTY

Talia and I spent another hour at Gino's, but I probably wasn't the best of company. I kept rolling around in my head the conversation with Marlow, and something just didn't feel right. From a distance, he reminded me of the cliched, good ole' boy who had wandered up from the Ozarks and somehow made good. In person he'd come across as softer, almost squishy.

Talia picked up on my mood when I returned to the table and kept the conversation light, giving me plenty of quiet moments. When we finished, I walked her out to her Nissan, parked around the corner, and reaffirmed plans for the next weekend.

From the northern part of downtown where Gino's is located, it's only about a ten-minute drive to my place. The sun had gone down about an hour before, but, as usual with Missouri summers, full darkness hadn't yet descended. Pulling into a parking space next to my apartment building, I could clearly see a silver Corvette parked half a block down the street.

Turning the Cherokee off, I climbed out, crossed my arms, and leaned against the fender well.

A minute later, the 'Vette's driver door opened up and James Ericson climbed out.

"Interesting company you keep," he called out as he walked up to me.

"Talia?" I said. "She's the best."

Ericson shook his head. "Not who I meant, man, and I think you know it."

I uncrossed my arms to show him I had nothing in them. "You been following me?" I asked.

Ericson grinned. "Uh uh."

Comes the light. "You've been following Marlow. Dogging him around and saw him talking to the PI you came across in Laura Mosby's house the other day."

"Yep," Ericson said.

"Isn't that a little dangerous?" I asked. "Following someone as high profile as him?"

Ericson cocked his head and gave me a look. "I'm surprised, Quinton. Not the question I expected you to ask."

"Oh? And what did you expect?"

He grinned, and his entire body seemed to loosen up. "I figured you'd want to know exactly why I'm birddogging Marlow."

"It was going to be my next question."

Ericson chuckled. "Looks like the two of us are chasing opposite ends of the same snake."

"Lt. Santiago, down at headquarters. He'd probably be interested in talking to you."

"I'm sure he would," Ericson said, "but then he'd ask all kinds of questions. Such as who my client was and stuff like that I can't answer."

"I'd still kind of like to find that out myself."

Another chuckle, almost a laugh this time, before Ericson turned his back to me. "Have a good night, Quinton. Not wanting to cause trouble. Just want to make sure we don't cross each other too much."

"I'll do my best," I said to his retreating back.

After the silver 'Vette fired up and roared away, I spent about a minute trying to put all the pieces together.

Didn't succeed, so I said to hell with it and went inside for the night.

CHAPTER THIRTY-ONE

ONE THING SEEMED OBVIOUS FROM MY MEETING with Marlow and the interaction after with Ericson. Whatever was going on, it was much more than a simple murder case. More than that, I'd heard whispers of Marlow's "handlers." I figured it was time to try to nail down just who it was.

The next morning, I called Josh Nichols at home. The detective sergeant usually left his house around seven, so I made sure and buzzed him at a quarter till. Not a problem because Josh and I were best buds.

"I probably shouldn't be talking to you, Blondie," Nichols said upon answering the phone.

See, buds.

"Maybe I just wanted to say good morning," I said.

"Good morning and goodbye."

"What's with the attitude, guy?" I asked.

A pause, an indecipherable mumble, and I could picture Nichols shaking his head. "You really know how to stir things up, don't you?"

"Can I assume you're referring to my meeting with the mayor last night outside of Gino's?"

"You can so assume. How long did you think it would take before word got around the department?"

"Honestly, Josh, I didn't really think about it. If the word's accurate, you should know the mayor came looking for me."

"All anyone knows for sure is you ended up in his car talking in private. Now half the force thinks you're on his pad somehow."

"What's the other half think?"

"Come on, Blondie."

"Don't come on Blondie me, Josh. I know you weren't kept directly in the loop, and that may be what has you so pissed off. You're smart enough to have a good hunch what last night concerned."

A couple of seconds of heavy breathing before Nichols answered. "A pretty good hunch, yeah."

"So how about cutting an old friend a little slack, and assume that Marlow came looking for me, not the other way around."

"So assumed. And I'm guessing, seeing as I was out of the loop there, that last week at some point Santiago came to see you because he had a little problem that was kind of delicate to handle within the department."

"I can neither confirm nor deny," I said.

"Uh huh. Christ, Blondie, you know how small this town is. Don't you know for the last day or so there's been all kinds of rumors circulating about you and the mayor?"

"Actually, I'd kind of hoped for that. But it's not why I'm calling."

"Oh? Then why are you?"

"'Cause I need some inside info, and I can trust you to keep it on the hush hush."

"Why don't you call your client and ask him?" Nichols said.

"I'm guessing that right at the moment he has his hands full. Matt Reynolds and Abbie Krenshaw are probably jumping all over him to let them go after Marlow, right?"

Nichols exhaled in frustration, and it almost sounded like a tornado coming my way. "This is a hell of a mess, Blondie. We've got cops wanting to haul the mayor in for questioning, and said mayor picking you up off the street for a powwow."

"Not to mention your boss withholding key information from his detectives, right?"

"Which I'm guessing is why he hired you," Nichols said. "To assist in nailing down that key info?"

"That was the general idea, though it obviously didn't go as planned."

"Not necessarily your fault, guy," Nichols said. "Though it is putting the department in a hell of a bad light."

"I'm sure. Damned if you do and—"

"Yeah, that's pretty much it. What'd you and Marlow talk about last night, or is that covered under client confidentiality?"

"Not at all. His Honor wanted to know why I was asking around town about him."

"Uh huh. I kind of wondered about that too, buddy. You're usually better at hiding your tracks."

"What's you're impression of him?" I asked.

"You mean as a politician, administrator, or potential murderer?"

"How 'bout all three?"

Nichols chuckled. "How about damned effective, passable, and I just don't see it."

I took a moment to ponder over what Nichols had said. "That's pretty much my gut feeling, buddy, especially after meeting him last night."

"Which leaves one pretty big question, doesn't it Blondie?"

"It does," I said, thinking of James Ericson and wondering just how he tied into all this. "Marlow's involved somehow. Question is how?"

"Yeah," Nichols said. "And if he didn't kill the girl, who did?"

CHAPTER THIRTY-TWO

A ROUND EIGHT THAT NIGHT, I TOOK my first step towards try-ing to pin down Marlow's clout by stepping into The Double L, a dive bar on the outskirts of town. Unlike the movies, conver-sation didn't stop as soon as I crossed the threshold, though I did notice one or two guys turning to eye me.

A twinge of nostalgia hit me. I'm old enough that I can remem-ber when you would walk into a bar or pool hall and be engulfed by a cloud of cigarette and cigar smoke. I never smoked myself, except for one or two experiments as a kid. One thing you learn early on in pro wrestling, if you're going to survive, is the most important part of your body isn't the biceps or the quads, it's the heart and lungs. As a result, tobacco and I have only the most dis-tant of acquaintanceships.

Even so, it just didn't seem right to walk into a bar, especially a working-class bar, and not have to dodge clouds of carcinogens. Now, we have a city ordinance, like most places, and progress trudges on.

'Course, there are still plenty of places around Providence where you can inhale to your heart's content, and every now and then I hear whispers about some of the uniformed cops being bought off to look the other way at a few of those places. The Double L wasn't that sort of place. Despite being filled with rough-looking guys, nary a peep of smoke to be found.

I nodded to the bartender, a tall, lanky guy with dark red hair. He nodded back even though, to the best of my memory, we didn't know each other. For the one or two men giving me a hard eye, I gave them one right back, and after a few seconds they turned and went back to their beer, their main preoccupation for the night.

The Double L is a squat, one-story establishment. Bar in front with tables and booths going all the way to the back. The rear of the building contains the bathrooms and a couple of old pinball machines with half their lights burned out.

The farthest back of the booths was my destination.

They were waiting for me when I got there. Not that they knew I was coming ahead of time. Rather, it was their job to be ready for anyone or anything to come along. Two toughs who could have stepped right out of a Martin Scorsese film, complete with tight tee-shirts with pockets on the chest, slicked-back black hair, and three-day growths of beard.

I paused for a moment, realizing that, except for the greasy hair, they pretty much resembled younger versions of myself. I didn't have long to consider that, though, before the lone guy sitting in the booth spoke up.

"Well, I'll be damned. Looks like someone needs a favor."

Sean O'Flaherty is a true-blue Irishman, though he operates as the local man on the Providence scene for the Chicago mob. A little under six feet, he keeps himself in good shape. Mid-fifties at my guess, he has slightly thinning light blond hair and a pair of the brightest blue eyes I've ever seen.

"I don't know about a favor," I said, "but if you have a minute, Sean, I'd like to talk to you."

O'Flaherty grinned, showing perfectly-capped teeth. Their brightness complemented the navy-blue suit and solid maroon tie he wore. At a guess, I'd say the tie alone cost about as much as the monthly rent on my apartment, and I figured if I knew the price of his suit I'd probably start hyperventilating.

"What the hell," he said. "It's been a slow night. Have a seat, Quinton."

I bellied my way into the opposite side of the booth while O'Flaherty waved his hand at the two bruisers. They moved off a ways, far enough to be out of ear range yet close enough to come back in a flash if their boss needed them.

I hoped he wouldn't. O'Flaherty and I are about as far as possible from being friends, if for no other reason than that it's not helpful to the health of an investigator's license to hang around with known criminals. He'd been in the Providence area for going on a couple of years now, having replaced the late, unlamented Paddy O'Brien.

We'd met about half a year ago, when I'd discovered him lurking around the periphery of the Felix Thayer case. Despite our differences, and the fact a lot of my friends on the force would like to put him behind bars, O'Flaherty and I had found ourselves having to work together.

"I'm kind of surprised you're operating so out in the open," I said.

O'Flaherty raised his hands in a kind of half shrug. "You call this out in the open?" he asked.

"Beats a social club on Mott Street in Brooklyn," I said.

The mobster grinned. "That it does. What can I do for you, Quinton?"

"Need to talk about politics."

"One of my least favorite subjects," O'Flaherty said. "What the hell, I got nothing else going on for an hour or so. You want a drink?"

"No thanks," I said. "I'd prefer to keep my wits about me."

O'Flaherty grinned and, catching the eye of his two toughs, pointed to his almost-empty mug. One of the goons nodded and headed off to the bar.

"So what's shaking in the world of politics?" O'Flaherty asked.

"Bob Marlow," I said.

"Our esteemed city father," O'Flaherty said.

"Someone has strings on him."

The Irishman nodded. "Naturally. If someone's in the power structure, whether local, state or federal, someone's got strings. So what?"

I considered debating O'Flaherty's cynical view of public life but knew he was probably right. "The strings yours?"

Goon Number One returned from the bar and placed a full mug in front of his boss, removed the empty, then moved off again. O'Flaherty took a long swallow, draining a third of the glass, before putting it down and looking my way.

"Couple of options come to mind here," he said.

I nodded and waited for him to continue.

"Option number one is you came in here tagged by the cops 'cause they're wanting to get something on me."

I took a deep breath. "I guess that would be a possibility to consider."

O'Flaherty peered at me a little closer. "It don't quite seem right, though. Just because we did a little business together a while back doesn't exactly make us buddies, you know?"

"I do."

"Plus, cops don't usually use private hires for their work. Leads to all sorts of problems if things get into court."

"Especially if someone has good lawyers, like you," I said.

O'Flaherty nodded. "True."

I began breathing a little easier. "What's option number two?"

He took another long drink from his mug before setting it down and using a napkin to wipe his mouth. "Option two is you're working for some other—ahh—businessmen and trying to pull something over."

"I can see how that would be a little more likely," I said.

O'Flaherty shook his head. "That one doesn't really wash either."

"Good to know. How come?"

The Irishman smiled. "Because I know all the people in the area who would possibly be inclined to pull something like that."

"Always good to know your competition."

O'Flaherty frowned. "I didn't say they were competition, Quinton. Providence may seem like the small time, but you and I both know who's backing me. People like that don't have real competition. Don't believe all the crap you hear about how times are changing. When it comes right down to it, the boys are still the main game in town. And when competitors show up, they tend not to stay alive too long."

"Point taken," I said.

"Then the only thing that leaves me with, especially knowing you, is you're trying to help somebody out of something."

"That would be more likely," I said, "considering it's kind of my profession."

O'Flaherty leaned back and clasped his hands on the table in front of him. Off to the side, his two guys were still standing like statues. The low-key murmuring of a bar full of people trying to while away the hours provided background noise.

"You did right by my cousin," the Irish gangster finally said.

I felt a bit of a lump in my throat. "Didn't do much in the long run to help her."

O'Flaherty nodded. "No, you didn't. On the other hand, neither did I, and it was my job to watch out for her, not yours."

Although I didn't quite remember our last encounter that way, I didn't see the point in arguing.

"You know," O'Flaherty said, "there was a time early on there, when I wasn't sure about your involvement with her, and I was seriously considering having one of the guys take you out."

Not exactly news to me.

"In the end," O'Flaherty said, "I was glad I didn't."

"Me too," I said.

O'Flaherty stared at me for a minute, then picked up his mug and drained his drink. He put the mug back down and wiped his lips again.

"We've got no strings on Marlow."

I sat up a little straighter. "None at all?"

"None."

"A bit odd," I said, "considering he's the mayor and all."

"True. Problem is he's the mayor of Providence, while Jeff City is right down the road."

"Why bother with one dinky little town when you've got the state capital close by," I said.

O'Flaherty nodded. "Exactly."

"You're saying Marlow would be small potatoes for you guys."

"Correct."

"For anyone else?" I asked.

O'Flaherty signaled to his bully boys, and one of them went off to the bar again. "Meaning would anyone else be holding those strings you're interested in?"

"Yep."

He waited until his guy came with a fresh drink and moved off before answering. "I can think of one or two who might. Why all this interest in the mayor?"

If I tried to pull the old "client confidentiality" bit, O'Flaherty would only laugh. And maybe ask his boys to beat me up. Although I questioned that they could, why go through the hassle? Besides, I didn't feel the need for a workout this late in the evening.

"I can't say for sure," I said. "If things go the way I expect, you may be hearing about it in the media before too long."

O'Flaherty lowered his mug to the table and peered at me. "Now that's kind of interesting."

"And," I said, "even if you don't really see them as competition, wouldn't hurt for some of them to be out of your way, would it?"

"I don't think it would mean anything to my sponsors back in Chicago. Could make things a little easier for me on a day to day basis. Not a lot, but a little."

"Then how about giving me some names?"

He did the peering thing again before settling back in his seat. "Why the hell not?" he said. "Worst can happen is a bit of discomfort for some people I don't care for. But how do you know what I give you will be the straight stuff?"

"Come on, Sean," I said. "You've been a crook your whole life, and on top of that you're the point man in Missouri for the Chicago Outfit."

"Yeah?"

"With all that," I said, "would you lie to me?"

O'Flaherty smiled. "You got a point."

He reached into his pocket and pulled out a small notebook, produced a pen, and wrote something on one sheet of the notebook, which he tore out and slid across the table.

"There's a name may interest you," he said.

I folded the paper and put it in my jeans pocket without looking at it, then stood up. "Thanks, Sean. I hope this doesn't involve any quid pro quo on my part."

The mobster chuckled. "You mean like now you owe me a favor? Come on, Quinton. How many bad movies you seen?"

"Hopefully, too many," I said as I gave him an imaginary tip of the hat and walked out.

CHAPTER THIRTY-THREE

T HE NEXT MORNING, someone took a run at me.
I'd just left my apartment and had pulled the Cherokee up to the first stoplight at the corner. With the light red, I sat and started flicking the radio around to find some music that matched my mood.

A once-black but now primered Chevy Nova, from somewhere around the late seventies, pulled up in the lane next to me, muffler blapping. I glanced over at the two young kids in the front seat, who looked to be out of juvenile delinquent central casting.

The light turned green. As I eased into the intersection, I saw a flicker of light out of the corner of my eye. I glanced all the way over in time to see the Nova's driver, a pimply, red-headed guy, lifting a chrome-plated pistol into target acquisition.

I flicked my eyes both ways, then gunned the accelerator and shot all the way into the intersection. The Nova accelerated behind me, but I had enough lead room to slam on my brakes, yank the wheel to the right, and cause the Cherokee to whip around broadside to the Nova.

The driver must have been new to this kind of game because he tried slamming the brakes and yanking his wheel at the same time, which made his car almost smash nose first into the Cherokee's side. Somehow, he managed to turn it just enough that it ended up almost, though not quite, brushing paint with my vehicle.

Peering through the windshield, I saw the two youngsters splayed every which way and decided to take a chance and, their weapon notwithstanding, leave my gun behind in the car. If I drew my piece, things could get quickly out of hand, and I didn't fancy spending the next two weeks explaining to some bureaucrat why I felt it necessary to pull out a weapon in broad daylight.

I didn't know if the goon in the passenger's seat was armed or not, so I went first to the driver's side. The driver was a fat-faced blond kid, and by the time I got around the Cherokee's nose and alongside of the Nova's drivers side, he had pretty much oriented himself and jerked his door half open.

I didn't care much for that idea, so with as much oomph as I could put into the move I slammed the door right back shut.

Or almost shut. There was a small obstruction in the form of a halfwit, wannabe gangster between the door and the jamb. I didn't let it bother me. The kid screeched out in about the highest voice I've ever heard this side of a kindergarten classroom, and I put a stop to the noise by throwing a short, wicked hook straight at the side of his head.

As the punch slammed him back and down, I reached in and pulled the cheap chrome pistol out of his hand, then raced around to the Nova's passenger side. From the corner of my eye, I noticed a gray Camry screeching to a halt alongside of us, but didn't have time to worry about something new right then.

The passenger had managed to get his balance and wriggle out of the car. He met me halfway with another pistol rising. I put on a burst of speed and got to him before he could get the weapon all the way up, then slammed my forearm straight down on top of his arm.

The gun clattered to the pavement as I gave the punk an old-fashioned, straight of the hand chop across the chest. While not the most effective of moves in a street fight, when it comes at you from someone who outweighs you by fifty pounds or so, it does the job.

While I could have chopped just as hard on his throat, I wanted him out of the action, not dead.

I stooped down and gathered the gun, then as I turned to pick up the other one the door of the Camry opened up.

"This a usual kind of workout for you?" Det. Abbie Krenshaw said as she got out of the car.

CHAPTER THIRTY-FOUR

"**T**HANKS FOR JUMPING into the thick of it," I said.

Detective Krenshaw grinned, though the expression didn't have much humor behind it. "Hell, you were doing okay. Good enough you may rank as an actual tough guy someday."

It was about thirty minutes after my little encounter with the two hooligans in the Nova. Krenshaw had produced a couple of pairs of handcuffs, read the two their rights, then called in for a patrol car to come pick them up. I'd watched all this carefully, ready to run if she pulled out a third pair of cuffs.

Two must have been her limit for the day.

When the patrol car had arrived, Krenshaw had gone off to talk to the officers, leaving me leaning against the Nova's fender. The two kids glared at me the whole time. I smiled back. I would have loved to question them but figured it would have thrown Krenshaw over the edge.

Once the patrol officers had trundled the brats off to headquarters, Krenshaw turned to face me head on. "Ready to tell me what that was all about?" She held a small black notebook that she'd been taking notes on.

I spread my arms out, palms up. "Were you tailing me?"

"Huh?" A wary look came into the detective's eyes.

"Town's small, but it's not that small, Detective. The odds of you showing up just as a couple of gonzos jump me is a bit much. Were you following me?"

Krenshaw's expression flamed up for a moment, then cooled back down. "As a matter of fact, I was."

"Let me guess," I said. "My meeting with Marlow touch this off?"

"Not just that, Quinton. Though there's not much else being talked about in the department. When you take your hobnob with the mayor, plus his DNA being found at a murder scene, combined with Reynolds and me catching you lurking around that same murder scene, you can see how it would all come together."

I didn't really have anything to say, mainly because I saw her point. Until things broke one way or the other concerning the mayor, Lt. Santiago still had to keep his people covered as much as possible. Ergo, the idea that he'd hired a private eye to do what should have been city business had to remain in the Top-Secret category.

Instead of arguing with Krenshaw, I shifted gears. "Who were those two?" I asked as I jerked my thumb in the direction the squad car had taken.

"Pretty much the lowlifes they look like," Krenshaw said. "Richie Jenkins and Bobby Mosler."

"Connected to anyone?" I asked.

"Couple of pool hall hangers-on more than anything. Wave a hundred-dollar bill in front of them and they'll bend over and ask what color."

I frowned at her crudity. "So why'd they come after me?"

"Who knows?" Krenshaw said. "Look at it this way. It's lucky for you I was tailing you. I could clearly see it as self-defense on your part."

"I noticed you didn't have the uniforms haul me off as well. This mean you think I'm one of the good guys?"

Krenshaw had thawed for a few seconds there. Now the frost started to come back into her look and tone. "Not hardly. What it means is that, much as I don't want to, I can clearly see you were the aggrieved party in this little soiree. You hanging out with any lowlifes lately, besides the mayor? Anybody else you've pissed off besides us cops?"

"Had a talk with Sean O'Flaherty last night," I said.

Krenshaw's frost turned into a sour expression. "I haven't been in Providence long, Quinton, but it doesn't take much time to learn who the players are. Your talk with O'Flaherty friendly or acrimonious?"

"If I understand what you mean by acrimonious, I'm going to say it was very friendly. Still, you can't ever tell for sure what Sean will or won't do."

"That's what I hear."

"Then again, I'd like to think Sean has enough respect for me that if he did send someone after me, he could do a little bit better than those two sluggards."

Krenshaw sighed and put her notebook into her jacket pocket. "Maybe he doesn't have as much respect for you as you think. Come along sometime today to give us a statement, okay?"

Something occurred to me as Krenshaw climbed into her car. "Hey, Detective?"

She turned back. "What?"

"Where's your partner?"

A grunt, fairly low on the register. "Like you said, Quinton. I'm Reynolds's partner, not his babysitter."

And she fired up her engine and drove away.

CHAPTER THIRTY-FIVE

ABOUT AN HOUR LATER, I pulled into a parking spot outside a building on Main Street on the western edge of downtown. The McClurty Building had been part of the Providence cityscape for going on fifty years, and like most downtown construction from back in the old days, it only stands three stories tall.

There's a fine old hotel, smack dab in the middle of downtown, which boasts a huge sign bearing the name of the local university's mascot in bright red letters that light up at night. Once upon a time, actually not all that long ago, you could see the sign from practically any spot in the area, especially at night, mainly because of a strict zoning ordinance that didn't allow buildings downtown to exceed five stories in height.

But some years back, fueled by a sudden spurt of enrollment in the town's various colleges and an overall growth in population, the city council got wobbly, and before long they allowed construction of numerous parking garages, scattered throughout the downtown area, many of them tall enough to begin cutting off the view of the glorious old hotel sign.

Fortunately, so far the laxness in zoning hadn't extended to anything beyond parking garages, and all the office and commercial buildings still hovered in the two to four story range.

I'd only been in the McClurty Building a couple of times over the years, on odds and ends of business. With only three floors to the place, not to mention the large, brass-framed directory just to the right as you walked in the door, even a low-end snooper like me could find the suite of offices I was looking for.

As soon as I came off the staircase and entered Suite 3A, I knew I hadn't quite dressed for the environment. The outer office was all dark oak, polished metals, and wide, spacious windows. Each corner had a large plant growing in a receptacle, the floor was some type of hardwood I couldn't even identify, and a long, modernistic receptionist counter held two high-end Macs and one really well-put-together receptionist.

"Can I help you?" she asked, looking up from one of the Macs. She appeared half Asian, half Caucasian, and her glistening black hair somehow perfectly complemented the office décor. She wore a tan blouse, the top two buttons open, with a thin gold chain hanging around her neck.

"Tyler Phelps," I said. "Is he in?"

The woman looked at me for a moment, no doubt hoping my faded Levi's, black tennis shoes, and blue tee-shirt were from some famous designer she'd never heard of.

If I told her my entire outfit came from Kohls, it would no doubt burst her bubble all the way.

"Do you have an appointment, Mr.—"

"Quinton," I said. "Sam Quinton. And no I don't."

She didn't give me a smile so much as a brief quirking of the lips. "Mr. Phelps is a busy man, and he doesn't see people without an appointment."

I gave her a smile back, though more of a one than she'd given me, and leaned in a bit. "I think he'll want to talk to me," I said. "Tell him it's about Laura."

Her face tightened, and I had the impression she was torn between ushering me right in or trying her hand at throwing me out herself.

For some reason, I had a hunch calling the cops wasn't even an option.

Of course, folks like Tyler Phelps had a lot more dangerous people they could call on than simple police

"Look," she said, smiling even more in an attempt to warm up to me, "if I let you go in there, Mr. Phelps is going to be really upset. He's right in the middle of an—"

"Let me guess," I interrupted, "important international phone call."

In the old days, they used to say someone was on long distance as a way of putting off unwanted visitors. Modern telecommunications pretty much ruined that old line.

Beneath the silk blouse, I could see her shoulders tighten.

"Buzz the man for twenty seconds," I said. "Tell him it's in regards to Laura, and I can guarantee he won't be upset with you. In fact, he'll probably be more upset if he finds out later, and he will, that I was here and was turned away."

Although I felt kind of bad at bullying someone who was just trying to do their job, the stakes made it necessary.

"I don't know much about my boss, sir, but I can tell you he's a happily married—"

"It's not that kind of thing," I interrupted her. I'd specifically avoided showing her my PI license so she wouldn't get the wrong idea. "I can assure you he will want to talk to me."

Her lips puckered, indicating my word was the last thing she'd put her faith in. The kid was in a bad spot, this whole little scene probably way out of the zone of her normal workday, or year for that matter. After a second, she reached down somewhere below the Mac, lifted up one of those little plastic headgear things, and placed it on her head.

Feeling crummy about browbeating an innocent person just trying to do their job, I walked about twenty feet away to afford her some slight amount of dignity as she interrupted one of the richest, most powerful men in the state of Missouri, if not the entire Midwest.

After a moment, I heard the slightest of clatters, which I assumed was her dropping the headset onto the desktop, and turned back around.

"Door at the end of the hall," she said, her tone almost wooden.

I imagined she'd gotten an earful from her boss before she could get a word in edgewise.

I wanted to make her feel better but couldn't think of a good way to do so. Instead, I nodded and went on my way.

I entered the office without knocking, noticing it was the only one of four office doors that didn't have a nameplate. Closing the door behind me, I gave the room a good once-over.

It was almost the exact opposite of the outer area, clearly decorated with an old-fashioned male sensibility. Lots of varnished wood, dark brown or black leathers, and a lineup of sporting trophies and framed pictures filling up a shelf to the right. The desk looked like maple and had an antique cigar box at one corner.

No windows, kind of odd for the top man's office, and the lighting, muted and indistinct, gave the place about as much illumination as on a gray, cloudy day right before a thunderstorm.

My gut tightened. This wasn't a place for conducting business so much as a space for the good old boys to get together and bitch and moan about the good old days and how modern America was going to hell in a handbasket.

The man in question was playing it cool. He sat behind his desk, staring straight at me with hands folded in front of him. He wasn't shuffling papers, talking on the phone, tapping at a computer, or doing anything that would indicate what a busy, complicated work day he had.

"Mr. Quinton," he said as I shut the door, motioning to one of three black leather chairs arrayed in front of his desk. "I've heard of you," he said as I sat down.

I gave him a puzzled look.

Tyler Phelps smiled back at me, resembling a barracuda coming off a hunger strike. "George and Mary Hampton," he said. "They were acquaintances of mine."

My mind flashed back about a year to the Hampton case, when I'd become entangled in a decades-old murder plot. "Acquaintances," I asked, "not friends?"

Phelps smiled further, the barracuda resemblance now even more striking. "I doubt that George and Mary Hampton had many actual friends."

"I for sure wasn't one of them," I said, slouching a bit and crossing one leg over the other.

"So I hear," Phelps said. "What can I do for you?"

"Thought that was obvious. Figured we could talk about Laura."

"And I thought I just made it obvious I agreed to see you because I've heard you name. Not because of some coded message about somebody named Laura."

He was a cool customer, for sure. If I didn't trust what Sean O'Flaherty had told me, I would have figured I was off base and already be planning my exit. I trusted O'Flaherty's information, at least as much as you could trust anything from a wise guy, and decided to stick it out.

"Laura Mosby," I said.

Phelps furrowed his brow and stared off in the distance. The guy could have given acting lessons.

"Oh," he said a few seconds later, putting on a good show of someone whose mind had suddenly cleared. "The young woman who was murdered a few months back."

"Exactly."

Now the brow furrow intensified. "I'm not quite sure what this has to do with me."

A bit of red had crept into his neck.

While I hadn't done so with the receptionist out front, I now pulled out my PI license and handed it over to Phelps. He took it, looked it over for a moment, then snapped the leather case shut and slid it back across his desk to me.

"As I said, I know who you are. I don't know for sure what your game is, mister, but I can guarantee you that if you're thinking of somehow tying me into that poor girl's death you'd better reassess the situation damned quick."

"Reassess," I said, leaning back in my chair. "That's a nice, business way of putting it. Almost makes it sound like we're negotiating a deal."

"Everyone's negotiating all the time," Phelps said. "It's what makes everything keep spinning. Wherever you got your information from, and whatever it is you think you may have, you're way off. And if you even breathe a word connecting me to that dead girl, you'll regret it very quickly."

I did my best to put forth a he-man smirk and slouched lower in the chair. Despite the attitude I was presenting, I kept my eyes on Phelps's hands, in case he tried something.

"How about connecting you with Robert Marlow?" I asked.

Phelps's eyes narrowed. "Excuse me?"

"You know, the mayor. Providence's answer to Big Bubba. Surely you know him?"

"Of course, I'm acquainted with Mr. Marlow. What does that have to do with . . ."

I sat up straight, and leaned forward. "Tell you what, Phelps. How about you quit shitting around? You're not just acquainted with His Honor. Way I hear it, he wouldn't be in office if not for you."

Phelps took a deep breath and exhaled deliberately. "I'm a rich man, and rich men tend to be interested in politics. It's not a crime to support local figures."

"Nope," I said, "but helping to cover up a murder is."

The man arched, as if a bolt of electricity had gone through him. If I hadn't dealt with so many good liars over the years, I'd almost have believed him.

"Wait a minute there, Mr. Quinton. Are you saying Mayor Marlow is somehow connected with the death of that girl?"

Shaking my head, I stood up. "Nice try, Tyler. You know damned good and well he was involved, mainly because you're the son of a bitch who yanked his chestnuts out of the fire."

"I don't know what you . . ."

"Now, those nuts are right back in the fire, and there's no way His Honor is going to be able to avoid the scandal."

Phelps stood up, keeping his hands pressed flat on his desk. His gaze burned into me. "I think that's enough, mister. I don't know exactly what you want, and I don't care. I know the mayor, but no more intimately than probably a couple of dozen other business people in town. We clear?"

I kept my shoulders slouched and looked down more at his desk than at Phelps, doing my best to give an impression of someone who'd been thoroughly cowed.

"And what's more," he continued, not giving me a chance to reply, "if you so much as utter a word tying me in any way to the sort of nonsense you just spewed, I can guarantee you're going to regret it. How would you like to find your entire life turned upside down by every agency in this state? To have the tax people breathing down your neck? Far as that goes, a fairly liberal interpretation of what's been said in this office could be construed as a threat against a potential governor. You want that on your back?"

I'd played out about as much rope as I'd intended but wanted to give one more little poke into the hornet's nest. "Sure you won't try something else?" I asked. "Like maybe sending a couple of young thugs around to blow me off the side of the road?"

I got a reaction, though not quite the one I'd intended. Phelps's brow furrowed, as if genuinely puzzled by what I'd said. He quickly shrugged it off and went back to his former stern city father mode.

"I don't know what you mean. You come around here again, you come anywhere near me or mine, and forget everything I just said. I'll make a phone call, and you'll be dealing with people a whole lot nastier than the tax folks. And they operate all the way over on the other side of the line."

I gave him my own attempt at a stern look before turning and leaving his office. I nodded to the receptionist, who gave me more of her impression of a frost giant as I walked by.

Thinking about it, I didn't blame her a damned bit.

A minute later, I was on the sidewalk outside of the McClurty Building and heading down the block to where I'd parked the Cherokee. As I walked, I went back over everything that had happened in that office.

Meanwhile, I kept my eyes peeled as I wondered how long it would be before someone, working either for Phelps, the mayor, or someone else, made the next run at me.

CHAPTER THIRTY-SIX

N O ONE CAME FOR ME the next day.
Or the day after that.

By Saturday morning, I was beginning to wonder if I'd miscalculated somewhere down the line. It seemed obvious to me that if Marlow had killed the Mosby girl whoever was pulling his strings would help him cover it up. When I threw myself so blatantly in Tyler Phelps's face, I was practically begging him to have someone take a run at me.

Even if Phelps was in the clear, I'd also come to the attention of the mayor himself, so surely His Honor or someone would take more interest in me.

So far, nada.

Josh Nichols advised me that Jenkins and Mosler, the two criminal geniuses who'd tried to waylay me Wednesday morning, had been bailed out, with a court appearance set some time in the next decade. When Nichols inquired as to who exactly had put up the bail, he got a judicial runaround and eventually gave up.

Nichols also informed me that Reynolds and Krenshaw had yet to bring the mayor in for questioning. I'd already been aware of that, mainly because there would be no way in hell to keep such a thing off the local news. He said they were covering as many of their bases as possible before taking the jump and hauling Marlow in.

James Ericson also seemed to have gone off the radar. The cops couldn't cast much of a net for him, seeing as so far he hadn't done anything they knew of even remotely illegal. Even so, a loose look-out was turning up no trace of the guy, and the current suspicion was he'd returned home, at least for a while.

I tried a couple of times to call Matt Reynolds, but every message went to voice mail. After the second time, I took a chance and reached out to Abbie Krenshaw, who reamed me out for calling her personal number and wanted to know how the hell I'd gotten it anyway.

"I'm a detective, Krenshaw. Finding stuff out is what I do."

"No, blundering your way through other people's cases seems to be what you do. What do you want?"

I thought about pointing out my blundering had set me up as a target to hopefully smoke out the guilty party but decided she probably didn't want to hear it. "I've been trying to get ahold of Reynolds, but he's not answering. You know where he is?"

It took her a moment. "We've been kind of working on different ends the last day or so."

"Huh?" I asked.

"He's been doing his thing, and I've been doing mine. Hoping to kind of meet in the middle. I haven't seen him since yesterday morning."

So much for that.

Over two days now, and nothing. No movement on the case at all.

I felt pretty sure Phelps was the main backer and string puller behind the mayor. While Sean O'Flaherty may be a lot of things, misguided and mistaken weren't among them. If he said the mayor was in Phelps's pocket, that's how it was.

That did not, of course, automatically mean Phelps was involved in the Laura Mosby killing, or the attacks on me, if in fact the two were related.

Saturday morning came around, and I was dressing to spend the day pretending like I was running my gym, when my phone rang.

The ID indicated Det. Sgt. Josh Nichols's number, and I felt a little twinge in my gut.

"Hello," I said, hoping the twinge was the result of the chorizo omelet I'd had for breakfast.

No such luck.

"I'm downtown," Nichols said. "You should probably come out."

Yep, definitely not the chorizo. "Where?" I asked.

"Ninth and 1. Get here quick as you can."

NINTH STREET IS ONE OF THE BUSIEST of the seven north-south streets in downtown Providence. And don't even ask why with seven streets the numbering begins with Fourth. I've lived here off and on for decades and still can't figure that out. Certain times of the year, Ninth is the busiest because within its length are probably more stores, restaurants, souvenir shops, bars, and cafes than in any other stretch of town.

If you start at Main Street and walk south on Ninth, before too long you hit a short alley that connects Ninth with the next street over, conveniently named Tenth, and some astute city planner in the past took the lazy way out and labeled this as Alley 1. It stretches not quite a block in length, and is home to a handful of small businesses that run a little more to the exotic than the standard fare. There's a tattoo parlor, a musical instrument repair shop, an honest-to-goodness old time shoe repair store, and an oriental noodle place.

Plus, of course and naturally, a coffee shop.

With this being early morning, I parked around the corner on Main rather than deal with the already-congested Ninth. A couple of minutes after parking my car, I entered Alley 1 to find a knot of cops and other official folks moving back and forth.

Most of the action seemed to be centered around the tattoo parlor, and I spotted Abbie Krenshaw, standing ramrod straight about twenty feet away, looking anywhere except at the cluster of activity.

The slight twinge in my gut from earlier became a throbbing.

Santiago was there, wearing a navy-blue silk suit with a dark maroon tie. He had the suit jacket buttoned, and in the morning sunlight I couldn't see a wrinkle in it.

Josh Nichols stood next to him, wearing blue jeans and a tan blazer.

Neither man looked very happy.

I walked past Krenshaw and tried to catch her eye, but she just turned away. Her jaws were clenched, her posture so stiff she looked ready to snap.

The blue jeans and tan tee-shirt she wore look like she'd slept in them.

Crime scene tape hadn't been set up yet, and as I got closer to the center of interest a young blond guy in uniform held up a hand to stop me. At a barked command from Nichols he stepped aside and let me get closer.

At this time of the morning, the tattoo parlor was shut down, most joints like that not opening up until late in the afternoon and closing shop around three or four a.m. Even if the place had been open, they wouldn't have had much business filtering in this morning, and not just because of the throng of police hanging around.

Matt Reynolds lay slumped in the parlor's doorway, a good chunk of his head blown away.

CHAPTER THIRTY-SEVEN

"**Y**OU STILL POKING AROUND on the Mosby deal?" Santiago asked me.

Myself, the lieutenant, and Nichols had moved off a little ways from the tattoo parlor doorway to have a little privacy. Santiago waved a hand flagging Det. Krenshaw over to join us, and after a moment of intense frowning she did so. The four of us now formed a little cluster at one end of the alley.

"Just a poke or two," I said. "And that's been a few days ago. Nothing much has come of it."

"Det. Krenshaw mentioned that a couple of thuggoes took a run at you the other day."

"They did," I said. "Did she also mention I had to handle them all by myself?"

"She reported the situation was secured in a reasonable amount of time," Santiago said.

"I guess that's one way of putting it."

"This happen before or after the pokes you mentioned?"

"After one but before the other," I said.

"Nothing since?" Nichols asked, his tone sounding almost hopeful. I grimaced at my friend. "No such luck, Josh. Sorry to disappoint."

"What was the next part of the plan?" Santiago asked.

"Tell the truth, Lieutenant, I wasn't sure. I made as big of a stink as I could and waited. Obviously, I've been waiting for some sort of reaction, but it's been a couple of days now, and no followup."

"Looks like you did get a reaction," Krenshaw said, "just not directed at you." Her gaze went over to her partner's body, the hub of furious action by the crime tech people.

I hesitated on that one. Far as I could see, there was nothing to directly connect a dead Matt Reynolds with the Mosby case. True, he was one of the primaries, but surely he had other things he was working on as well.

"He have anything going at the moment besides Laura Mosby?" I asked.

Santiago shook his head. "Nope. Right now, that was all he and Krenshaw were on."

Okay, so much for that idea.

"Still," I said, looking more at Krenshaw than Santiago or Nichols, "any evidence so far linking this to Mosby? After all, last I heard, the mayor's still walking around a free man."

All three cops glared at me, and I realized I'd brought up a sore subject.

"Nothing at the moment," Nichols said, "except for the coincidence of timing. And it seems a little more than coincidental we find Matt here dead only a couple of days after you began pushing buttons.'"

"Far as that goes," Krenshaw said, "we're doing what's called building a case against the mayor, trying to nail him down before we bring him in for questioning. You know, actual police type work as opposed to running around town shooting our mouths off."

"Point taken, Detective, but look at it this way. Let's say I've managed to generate some heat over the last couple of days. Doesn't it make sense that the last thing they'd want to do is murder a cop? If anything, that's going to bring even more attention to the thing they're trying to quiet down."

"Depends on whoever did this was thinking logically," Santiago said.

"Far as that goes," I continued, "could be this has nothing to do with his work at all."

"Come again?" Krenshaw said.

I spread my hands out at my sides. "How do you know it's not connected with something in his personal life? Someone who had a grudge against Matt for some reason."

"That's Detective Reynolds, mister!" Krenshaw snapped. "Not 'Matt.'"

"Sorry."

"Take it easy, Detective," Santiago said. "It's a valid question, and you know it." He turned a little more my way. "Far as we know right now, Reynolds had nothing going on that would lead to something like this. Naturally," now a bit of the tone got directed towards Krenshaw, "it's something we're going to look into."

While Krenshaw continued glaring at me, Santiago had developed a thoughtful look. "Now then," he said to me. "How about you explain to us just what sort of buttons you've been pushing, hmm?"

I thought it over and couldn't see any harm now in unloading. So as the crime scene folks that had been buzzing around earlier began stepping away to allow the EMT's to do their thing with the body, I filled the cops in on my visit to Tyler Phelps's office.

"Doesn't sound like anything that could throw back to Reynolds," Nichols said.

"How firm was your info?" Santiago asked. "Maybe someone steered you wrong."

"Trust me. The info was solid. The main person in town pulling His Honor's strings is Phelps. If anyone was trying any dirty tricks to help Marlow out, Phelps would know about it."

Almost in unison, all four of us turned back to watch the EMT's loading Reynolds's body into their van.

"Then who the hell did this?" Josh Nichols asked.

Right then, none of us had an answer.

CHAPTER THIRTY-EIGHT

A FEW MINUTES LATER, WITH NOTHING HELPFUL to offer and basically feeling in the way, I headed out. Intending to go on to The Blaster and get some work done, within half a block I knew my heart wasn't in it.

Matt Reynolds and I hadn't been friends. Acquaintances, sure. You could have even called us friendly acquaintances. But tried and true friends? Naw, not really.

Despite the possibility I raised back at the scene, it seemed obvious something to do with the Mosby case had caught up with Reynolds. The prospect of some other case he was working on being connected would have made sense in New York, Chicago, or St. Louis.

But not in Providence. While most people who lived in the small towns and rural counties around the area considered our big, bad city of a hundred thousand or so a total hotbed of crime and violence, that perception didn't stand up to the truth.

True, we had more violence than back in the days when I was growing up around here, though nothing compared to what most people in the surrounding areas believed.

After driving another block, a new line of inquiry came to mind, and I pulled into the nearest parking lot and got out my phone.

I pulled a card out of my wallet, stared down at it for a moment, then made the call.

It could be a total waste of time. Then again, one never knew until one tried.

"Ericson," the voice on the other end answered. "What do you want?"

"Need to talk," I said. "Soonest possible."

James Ericson took a moment before replying. "I'm free right now if you want. Think I can spare about half an hour."

"You close by?" I asked, doing my best to keep sarcasm out of my tone.

"Yep. Still enjoying the sights and sounds of your fair city. Plus, you got better restaurants than back home. What's up?"

"I think we need to get together. Something's happened, and at the very least your client, whoever the hell he or she is, should be made aware of it."

A hint of tension came into Ericson's voice. "Where do you want to meet?"

CHAPTER THIRTY-NINE

W E MET UP AT A McDONALD'S on the south side of town. When I pulled in, I saw Ericson's silver 'Vette parked right in front of the door. A heat wave had begun creeping into the area early in the morning, and the temps were hovering somewhere in the mid-nineties, yet the top on Ericson's 'Vette was down.

A real tough guy.

He was standing just inside the door, waiting on me, and when I walked in we walked up to the counter without saying anything. We both ordered large coffees and nothing else, eliciting a sigh from the early twenties guy working behind the counter.

A minute later he slid both of our coffees to us and, still not speaking, we made our way to an empty booth in the far back of the dining area and sat down.

"What's up?" Ericson asked after we'd both taken sips of our beverage.

"A cop named Matt Reynolds was killed sometime last night or early this morning," I said.

Ericson frowned as he took another swig of his drink. "Okay. This relates to me how?"

"He was one of the two primaries on the Mosby case."

Ericson nodded but didn't say anything.

"The case," I continued, "that for some reason has you hanging around here. I've still been trying to figure out why someone from a hundred miles down the road is up here looking into one of our murders. And please don't give me any nonsense about the family back in Ohio hiring you."

Ericson grinned, took a long drink that almost drained his cup, then set it down. "You jealous they went all the way down my way rather than hiring local talent?"

"I would be," I said, "if I believed a goddamned word of it."

Ericson shook his head and took another sip. "Way this is all breaking, seems to me it's pretty wrapped up. Whispers are going around that any time now your cops are going to haul the mayor in for questioning. Whoever hired me, looks like they've gotten their money's worth. And all without me doing all that much."

"You think so?"

"Sure," Ericson said. "Especially now, with a cop being killed? I'd say it's a full-court press from now on, so what's left for a lone PI like you or me to worry about?"

For the last several hours, I'd been wondering the same thing. My end was done; Santiago had cut me loose. Why keep chasing a dog that loads of other people were more qualified to catch?

"Maybe Matt Reynolds was a friend of mine. And maybe I'm not too fond of seeing my friends murdered."

Ericson shook his head. "Uh uh. Doesn't wash, man. It's a natural feeling, but you and I both know the cops are a lot more equipped to handle the job than you. Or even me for that matter. What's the real scoop?"

I looked down at my hands, which had clenched into fists on the tabletop. I squeezed as hard as I could for a moment, at the same time taking slow, deep breaths. Ericson gave me my space, and after a few minutes I felt a little better.

Not much, but a little.

"Fair enough," I said. "It could just be that I'm worried I'm in some way responsible. Maybe something to do with my poking and prodding led someone to get nervous, and for some reason I don't yet know Reynolds stepped into the line of fire."

He gave out a full, deep laugh, then settled back in his side of the booth. "What the hell? Like I said, it's all pretty much a wash now. No matter which way it goes, your boy Marlow's pretty much toast."

"Meaning what?" I asked.

"You follow state politics much, Quinton?"

I shook my head. "No more than I have to, to get through the day."

"The name Lou Sanders mean anything to you?"

I thought about it for a moment, then shook my head.

Ericson chuckled. "City councilman down from my neck of the woods. Comes from a fairly well-off family and has aspirations for higher office."

The light didn't exactly dawn, though it did flicker a little. "Would I be a good guesser if I assumed he belongs to the same political party as Marlow?"

Ericson practically gleamed. "That would be a good guess."

"Then I'm going to really go out on a limb and conjecture that he's also been thinking about running for governor."

Ericson didn't say anything. By this point his smile practically blinded me.

"So are you investigating a murder," I asked, "or doing opposition research?"

Another chuckle, and the Rolla detective spread his hands on the table. "Does it have to be one or the other?"

I skulled it over a bit more and began to think I had the picture. What had started out as murky and confused was coming into rapid focus. I could have gotten up and walked away right then, but why deprive the guy of the joy of seeing me work it out?

"So this Sanders character hired you to do oppo research for his campaign?"

"Could have," Erickson said.

"And I've determined on my own that Marlow has a thing for younger women, and until Laura Mosby came along he pulled most of his shenanigans out of town to keep things hushed up."

Ericson took one last drink of coffee, then put his cup down. "Sounds like the dude had a plan."

"Then how bouts I really go out on a limb and deduce that someone in your neck of the woods glommed onto Marlow's activities."

"Sounds to me like you may be a pretty good deducer."

I continued putting two and two together and eventually came up with somewhere around eight million. "This Sanders character sent you up here to get the goods on Marlow."

Ericson continued beaming as he nodded his head.

"Someone, or a bunch of someones, knew that Marlow was seeing Laura Mosby."

"Despite what I first thought," Ericson said, "I see you can do this detecting business."

"I have my moments," I said, "though I'm sort of wondering why you're being so forthcoming with me right now."

Ericson looked down at the table and swiveled his cup back and forth in his hands. "Maybe the murder of a cop kind of changes things. After all, the Mosby girl was killed before I ever got down here. Your friend happened in the here and now. Makes things a tad bit more immediate, if you get my drift."

I thought it through some more, taking up time by draining my coffee. Something still didn't add up, and I wasn't sure how to approach it without Ericson clamming up entirely.

He sat patiently, watching me, waiting for the next step in our dance.

Then it hit me, in an almost painful way, and I fought to keep Ericson from seeing me tremble a bit. "Laura Mosby's killing was big news here in Providence."

"No doubt," Ericson said.

I peered at him. "Wouldn't rate that much of a blip down your way."

"So?" Ericson asked, his face as smooth and noncommittal as ever.

"So how did your client notice it, let alone make the connection with Marlow?"

"I told you. We've been doing oppo on the guy. Got a list of three or four women he's danced around with. So what?"

"So how did you possibly know to come down here? Unless you had her name flagged somewhere or unless—" I stopped there, not wanting my brain to speed ahead of my mouth.

Ericson sighed, slumped his shoulders a bit, and nudged his empty cup to the other side of the table. "Like I said, man, enough of this. The killing of a cop changes things. No way I'm going to jeopardize my license for one client."

"A client who's politically connected, at least at the state level," I said.

"At the moment, there's about a dozen men and women dickering around for the party's nomination. But the truth is, at least according to current polling, it's really a question of either Sanders or Marlow."

"And Sanders is connected."

"Uh huh."

"In all sorts of places?" I asked.

"Pretty much." His blank look seemed to have the slightest bit of a strain to it.

"Including the state police crime lab?"

The blankness vanished, and Ericson began to grin. "You do have a bit of a brain on you, don't you Quinton?"

"Son of a bitch. This Sanders character got the word the same as Santiago."

"Maybe," Sanders said. "Actually, wouldn't surprise me if my client got the word even before your local cops did. Understand, that's strictly a guess on my part."

"But is it usable?" I asked.

"Meaning?"

"It proves Marlow was up to something with her. Doesn't prove he killed her."

Now, Ericson's smile practically split his face. "That's the beauty of the job, Quinton. In order to wipe Marlow out politically, don't have to prove anything. Just raise the possibility and public opinion will do the rest."

As I sat there and thought it over, I couldn't really disagree.

CHAPTER FORTY

THE WEEKEND WENT BY in kind of a blur. Talia was busy with some sort of administrative emergency at the university, probably some full professor lost a box of paperclips, and we talked once or twice over the phone. Sunday night we made a firm commitment to get together on Friday.

I stayed away from The Blaster the entire weekend, mainly because I didn't really feel like being around people. I cleaned my apartment top to bottom, a task about six months overdue, and spent Sunday evening splayed out on the couch, TV remote in hand, rarely staying on any channel more than three minutes before clicking on.

Somewhere around midnight I became nostalgic for the days when TV remotes actually clicked and realized just how out of sorts I felt.

I got up, turned off all the lights, and went to the living room windows to close the drapes for the night. I stood at the window, hand on the drapes cord, and looked out into the night.

I stood there for a minute, my eyes fixed on the parking lot below, then closed the drapes in as casual a manner as possible. Instead of heading to the bedroom, I walked over to the front door and eased my way out.

CHAPTER FORTY- ONE

MY APARTMENT IS LOCATED in an older neighborhood, set in a three-story house divided into six units, two to a floor. There's a small parking lot behind the house, and trees along the street give quite a bit of shade.

Especially at night, they provide enough shade that, after going out the back way, I managed to loop around and sneak up on the parked, gray Kia without a whole lot of effort. Coming alongside the car from the rear, I saw my first impression upstairs had been right, and the car only held one person.

Once I got close enough to see, I made a mental note of the license plate, just in case.

Setting out, I'd considered grabbing my gun but decided against it. Mainly because I didn't know the identity of the person watching my place and didn't want to cause any unnecessary ruckus in the neighborhood.

Plus, hardened criminals don't usually drive ten-year old, slightly-rusted Kia's.

Rather than try anything super sneaky, I walked straight up to the driver's side door and grabbed the handle. If it had been locked, I would have had a bit of an issue.

Turns out the occupant was so inept when it came to sneaky stuff that he hadn't even thought to lock the door. Simple matter then to whip it open, reach in, and yank him out by the neck.

The man let out one little squeak when I shoved him against his car.

I didn't do much more because right away I recognized him. "Raimes," I said. "What are you doing?"

CHAPTER FORTY-TWO

"**Y**OU USUALLY GO AROUND assaulting city employees?" Raimes asked.

"Better than assaulting folks who work for the county. Those guys are actually tough."

"Whatever." Raimes and I were sitting in his car, him in the driver seat and me in the passenger. He'd suggested going up to my apartment to talk. I'd vetoed that right away.

"Far as that goes," I said, "I'm not sure being a city employee allows you to be lurking around a private residence."

"I wasn't lurking. I'm parked on a city street." His brown eyes looked even more watery than they had the other day.

"At nighttime, for who knows how long without moving, and watching one particular home. That constitutes lurking in almost anyone's book," I said. "So what about it?"

Raimes heaved a sigh and rubbed his palms along his thighs. "The cops took the mayor in for questioning."

"I'd say it's about time."

"I bet you would." He tried to give a manly snicker but didn't quite pull it off. "You have anything to do with it?"

"Why do you ask?"

"Because you've been snooping around this whole thing for someone. Did you turn the cops onto the mayor?"

It seemed His Honor's network wasn't very good if his top guy didn't know the reason why Marlow got pulled in.

"I work under confidentiality agreements, Raimes. Won't be in business long if I go around blabbing my clients' business to everyone."

"So you say."

"Why are you here? Going to try to muscle me a second time?"

He looked out the windshield. I wasn't sure what he was looking at, as the street in front of us was dark and empty. "I guess I wanted to know if I'm working for a killer or not."

The words made sense, but the tone was off, as if he was reciting a rehearsed line. I had to remind myself that he worked for a politician, and it seemed pretty obvious he was following the time-honored practice of covering himself in case the boss went down.

I guess I could understand it, even if it made my gut curdle a bit.

"How long have you wondered?"

"Of course, I had to consider it when they hauled him in," Raimes said. "But I didn't put a whole lot of worry into it."

"Uh huh."

"Then I thought about that cop, the one who was working the case, ending up dead, and well, you know."

"No, I don't know. Why did that make you suspect your boss?"

"Think about it. A couple of days before they bring him in, one of the cops goes and gets himself killed? It's natural to wonder if two and two go together."

The guy had a point there.

I opened the door and got out. "Go home, Raimes. Starting tomorrow, go back to doing whatever it is you do at City Hall. Just leave me the hell alone."

I thought of slamming the door to make my point, but didn't.

Maybe I was finally growing up a bit.

CHAPTER FORTY-THREE

MONDAY MORNING, I DECIDED the hell with it, and after about an hour-long workout at home to purge Sunday's lazing out of my system, I went in to the gym to get some work done.

Santiago called me a little after ten. "Marlow's in custody."

I sat in my office for a minute and breathed deeply. "I heard. Solid?"

A pause came over the phone before Santiago replied. "As solid as can be."

"Which means you still only have the DNA," I said.

"That plus his general dickish behavior."

"Forgive me for asking, Lieutenant, but it's been a few years since high-school civics class. Does dickish behavior fall under probable cause?"

Another pause, more drawn-out this time, before the lieutenant spoke up. "Okay, so we don't have a whole hell of a lot, and for all I know his lawyer's down at the courthouse springing him right now. But dammit I had to do something to placate Krenshaw."

"I'm guessing still upset about losing her partner?"

"Wouldn't you be? It's only been a couple of days, so she's still kind of wired."

"Funeral planned yet?"

"I'm thinking end of the week. Haven't heard for sure yet."

For a minute, I drummed my fingers on my desk. "Is Krenshaw going to transfer to another city again?"

"Meaning?"

"Come on, Santiago, you know goddamned well what I mean. How bad is this going to come back on her?"

"The idea is that it won't. Any minute now, the news of Marlow's arrest is going to break, if it hasn't already, and there will be so much attention drawn on him he wouldn't dare try to have her fired."

"Sure," I said, "now. What about a month from now? Six months? Next year? Once he walks, because let's face it, all you have on him is evidence he knew the Mosby girl, not that he killed her. How are you going to protect Krenshaw's job once he's free and clear? Or your job for that matter?"

The silence from the other end of the phone was practically venomous. I waited, almost thinking Santiago had hung up, before he spoke again.

"What's it to you?" he said. "I hired you for a piece of work, and you did it the best you could, but it's past you now. So what do you care?"

I started to say something, then realized I didn't have an answer for him. The cop was right. My part in this was over, or would be as soon as Santiago somehow managed to pay me for the rest of my time. I'd done the best I could. Wasn't my fault the damned DNA matchup got leaked before I had a chance to make much headway.

I could tell him I thought he was a good cop and I hated to see him hang himself out like this, though I wasn't even sure about that. For all I knew, his song and dance at the beginning about wanting to protect his people was only a way of masking that it was his job and career he was worried about.

Or I could say I was worried about dropping the ball with Reynolds when, in an indirect way, I'd been hired to safeguard the two cops. Now here Krenshaw was dangling on a hook, and Matt Reynolds was down at the mortuary.

"I guess I feel like I came up short," I finally said.

"Don't worry about it. Happens to the best of us," Santiago said before hanging up.

Sure, happens to everyone.

Didn't make me feel a whole lot better.

CHAPTER FORTY-FOUR

I SPENT MOST OF THE DAY PUTTERING AROUND, generally making a nuisance of myself to my staff while trying to put the Mosby affair out of my head. Didn't hear anything more from Santiago, which kind of surprised me, nor from Krenshaw, which didn't surprise me at all.

Sometime after noon I thought of calling Josh Nichols to see how things were going with the interrogation of the mayor, then figured I'd butted in enough over the last few days. I didn't for a minute believe any of my actions had led to Matt Reynolds being executed in that alley, but I couldn't keep myself from feeling a little guilty.

Shortly after five, I decided to call it a day and head home to grill up a steak. I hoped the looks of relief I saw on Lisa and Keri's faces as I headed out were my imagination.

I'd made it halfway to my Cherokee when a blond-haired guy who looked like a retired linebacker intercepted me. He didn't put hands on me or anything, just clearly stepped in my way.

"You Quinton?" he asked as he stared me down. The guy was wearing black slacks, a white polo shirt, and black light-weight leather jacket.

Seriously? A leather jacket in the tail end of June?

On top of that, the garment was cheaply made and didn't do much to conceal the gun tucked in the guy's waistband.

By this point, I was sick and tired of large guys, no doubt

working for powerful guys, thinking they could throw their weight around. I drew myself up my full height and nodded.

The side of beef took three steps closer, putting himself clearly in my personal space. "Someone wants to talk to you," he said.

Looking off to my right, I saw a familiar-looking limousine taking up three parking spaces, one of them a handicapped spot.

"No problem," I said, "but there's one thing I have to do first."

"What's that?" Beefcake asked.

I took a step forward and to the side of him, as if to walk around, then pivoted sharply on my left foot. Before the dude could so much as blink, I pistoned my right fist into his kidney.

He doubled over, though not all the way. He grasped his knees and began to stand back up when I rabbit punched him on the back of the neck, which put him down for good. He raised up about an inch off the pavement, grunted, then collapsed back to the ground.

I continued in the limo's direction. I half wondered if it would start up and drive away. Instead, it just sat there.

Wondering if I'd have to pull a real cave man act, I grabbed one of the rear door handles. Unlocked, it came straight open.

Bending down, I looked inside and, yep, sure enough, there he was waiting on me.

One thing I knew for sure without bothering to check with the cops.

Somehow, Bob Marlow had gotten himself released.

CHAPTER FORTY-FIVE

THE MAYOR LOOKED A LITTLE DIFFERENT than the last time I saw him. His clothes, including shirt with open collar and wrinkled slacks, appeared to have been slept in. His graying hair was limp and greasy looking. His eyes were bloodshot, and as he sat back and crossed his hands over his lap, they shook a bit.

His face was loose and flabby with a sagging double chin.

Seems spending several hours in police custody didn't quite agree with the man.

Not sure where this was leading, I scooched into the limo and took a seat as far from him as possible. I didn't expect any physical danger, the groaning oaf out on the pavement had pretty much settled that, but I still wanted some space between us.

"What do we need to talk about?" I asked.

Marlow quirked an eyebrow up, and something passing for a sick smile flickered across his face. "How's about shutting the door? I want this private."

"Even from Gomer out there?" I asked.

The mayor cast a disdainful glance at his henchman, now starting to get to his knees. "Yeah, even from that fuckup. Maybe especially from him if that's all the good he is."

Shrugging, I leaned over and shut the door, then stared the mayor down.

"Not using cops as your gophers anymore?" I asked.

He tried to give me a big, booming smile. When I kept my face straight, he gave up and collapsed back into his seat. "Bet you're surprised to see me out and about, huh?"

"Not really," I said. "I figured you'd be able to slime your way out before long."

"Now that hurts, Quinton. Slime my way out implies I'm guilty. What if I'm innocent of that poor girl's murder?"

I shrugged. "Guess that's for a jury to decide."

"No, goddammit, it's not for a jury to decide." A bit of fire had come back into his eyes. "Mainly 'cause it's never going to get that far. The cops don't have a goddamned thing on me, and they know it. I'm just waiting on the phone call from the DA telling me he told Santiago and his crew to go stuff it."

"Nice way you have there of relating to your city employees."

The flame in his eyes flickered, died out, and he slumped even further back into his seat. "Dammit," he muttered, and it seemed more to himself than to me, "I never wanted any of this."

"Any of what?" I asked.

I was curious. Sue me.

He lifted his right hand and waved it around. He appeared to be indicating the interior of the limo, but I got the feeling he was imagining a much larger area. "This," he said. "All this stuff. I just wanted to be the mayor, have some fun on the side, and let life go on."

Now I was really curious. "What about the governorship?"

He snorted. "You serious? Why the hell would I want that much hassle? Sure, I could move down the road to Jeff City and the big house. And for what? To have people bothering me twenty-three hours out of every day instead of only twenty-one? To have to deal with all those yuk-yuks in Washington? No thanks."

I stared at Marlow, trying to figure out if he was on the level or not. His general expression appeared one of disinterest, though somewhere deep in the eyes I thought I made out a little regret.

Through the tinted window, I could see the muscle boy bouncing back and forth on his feet, his fists clenched at his sides.

Marlow pressed a button to roll down my window and waved the guy away.

"You don't want him to hear what we have to say?" I asked.

The mayor cracked a grin, though not much of one. "Forget that. I don't want him to take another shot at you. You may get annoyed and really hurt him."

"You should hire a better quality of thug," I said.

Marlow looked hard at me for a second. "Who says I'm the one who does the hiring around here?"

He gave me an opening there, which I decided not to pursue at the moment.

"If you're not interested in the governorship," I asked, "why are you running?"

Marlow grimaced, and the regret in his eyes was replaced by something else. "What all work have you done in your life, Quinton?"

Puzzled, but not wanting the conversation to end in case it revealed something, I began ticking off on my fingers. "Swept floors and did general gopher work in an old boxing gym. Pro wrestler while doing odd jobs, then wrestling full time. Bouncer and assistant to a PI, up to now."

"And you've got two jobs, right? That gym of yours and your detective gig."

"That's right."

Marlow nodded. "A little out of the ordinary you'd say, but basically normal, upright work."

"If you say so. What's the point?"

A little red crept into the mayor's face. "The point is, I don't have an ordinary job. Haven't had for years. And when you get into the kind of circles I've run in for the last few decades, the kind of circles you have to run in if you're going to get in office, let alone stay there, you don't always get to choose where you go and what you do."

"You don't want to run for governor, but the people who pull your strings do, right?"

Marlow didn't say anything, just gave me blank look.

"People like Tyler Phelps?" I asked.

Marlow gave a little sigh and seemed to shrink in on himself a bit. His face got, if anything, even puffier than before.

I decided, what the hell, and went for the jackpot. "Did you kill Laura Mosby?"

He shook his head, and believe it or not, his eyes took on a shiny look. "No," he said, "I didn't, although for a while last night, tucked away there in the station, I thought about confessing."

"Guilty conscience," I asked, "because of your past?"

"Huh?" His eyes widened. "What do you mean?"

I took a moment, wanting to weigh my words carefully.

"You've got something of a history when it comes to women," I said.

Marlow nodded, and the confusion left his face. "Oh, sure. It's not exactly a secret that I tend to play the field."

A quick image came to mind of Ryan Granger mocking me for using the phrase "fooling around." What would the kid think about "playing the field?"

"You've got a bit more of a history than that, Mr. Mayor," I said.

He peered at me for a moment, as if trying to read my mind.

"You got a little rough with a girl one time," I prodded.

Marlow's face scrunched as he tried to remember.

I gave him the time he needed.

A moment later, his confusion cleared up. "The Rivers woman," he said.

I nodded. "Melissa Rivers."

"I got a little too drunk that night. I'll admit it. A little carried away. I'll tell you now, it wasn't the first time, but it was the last."

"How so?" I asked.

Marlow squirmed in his seat, like a little boy looking for the nearest bathroom. "That was the night I realized I was getting a little too old and had to start watching myself. I'll admit that I used to have fun getting a little rough, but never to the point that the woman objected."

I rather doubted the truth of that last comment, though could easily see Marlow believing it himself. "Until that night," I said.

Marlow nodded. "Until that night. I kind of scared myself then and made a vow to be more careful. I've been more careful ever since."

"Says you."

"Says me," Marlow agreed. "I'm not saying I'm a saint or any-thing, Quinton. But I'm telling you that I'm no killer."

Every instinct told me not to believe a word the man said. After all, he'd been a professional politician almost all his life. If he wasn't sincere, then the man should truck out to Hollywood and start an acting career.

"You knew Laura, though, right?"

He didn't exactly grin, but for a moment there his features seemed to lose some of their weight. "I'd say everyone and their dog knows about our little affair by now."

"You with her on the night she died?"

"You wired up in any way?" Marlow asked.

"Come on, mayor. Your nail chewer out there caught me com-ing out of my gym. I had no idea I was going to be shanghaied by you."

Marlow nodded. "Good point. Even so, for whoever may be listening, what I'm about to say in no way constitutes a confession to any illegal activity on my end. Got it?"

I sighed and considered seeing how many times His Honor would bounce if I threw him out the window. "Got it," I said.

"Yeah, she and I got together that night."

"And?" I asked.

"And what do you think, Quinton? Big guy like you, I got to draw you a picture?"

"No, but it would be nice to have the general outline filled in."

Marlow pushed a recess on the console between us, and reached into the space revealed to pull out a beer. Much as I wanted to snicker, I kept my face straight. In my reddest of redneck days, I never would have stooped to drinking beer out of a can in a limo.

He popped the top, took a guzzle, then set the can down and drew his hand across his mouth. "I'd offer you one, Quinton," he said. "The problem is, I don't really like you all that much."

"No problem," I said, "the feeling's pretty much mutual."

Marlow nodded, took another, even longer swig of his bever-age, then sat the almost-empty can down on the floorboard. "I was with her till around midnight or so," he said, "then I had to go home to play the dutiful husband."

The next question was almost too obvious, but I'd learned long ago to never leave any box unchecked. "She alive when you left?"

Marlow gave me a look, as if he couldn't believe I'd dared to ask him such a question, then slumped his shoulders and looked out the window at the parking lot. "Yeah," he said. "I went over there, we bounced around for a bit, then she started getting a little mouthy, and I said the hell with it and left."

I perked up. "A little mouthy how?"

The mayor half turned from me, like he was trying to hide something. At the same time, I was getting the oddest vibe from him, as if he was happy to finally be able to talk to someone about it. "She was getting tired," he said.

"Tired?"

He half turned back to me. "Of us sneaking around. Said she wanted to be something more than a quick lay whenever I felt like it."

I thought about what Ryan Granger and Kylie Rogers had said about Laura's ambitions.

"She want to get married?" I asked.

"Don't think it was that so much. She just wanted something more. As for me, I mean, come on Quinton. Look at me for a second."

I stayed silent. Sometimes it's best not to prod people, but to let them talk however they want.

"I'm over fifty. Fat and kind of sloppy. And believe it or not, I'm okay with that. Another reason I don't want to run for governor. Hate the idea of getting all slicked up all the time."

"But?"

"But you can see how far-fetched it is that a young girl like Laura would actually be attracted to someone like me."

"You're starting to break my heart, Mr. Mayor."

Marlow chuckled. "Yeah, I know it sounds like some kind of old country song. You can see how it would make me feel special a couple times a week to be with a kid like her. Little bit of a break from all the swampiness of City Hall."

"So when you say she wanted more—more what?"

"Aw hell, Quinton. I can't really blame her. The kid was a hair-dresser, for Christ's sakes. What would you guess she wanted?"

I knew, from my previous snooping around, but wanted to keep the man talking as much as possible.

"Probably some glamor, some excitement in her life. Something to make her feel special. Like all those female clients of hers with the fancy clothes and nice cars."

Marlow nodded, his extra chin wagging a bit. "That's exactly right. She wanted to be somebody, to be known. And the easiest way she could see to do that . . ."

"Christ," I said, the light finally dawning. "Was she blackmailing you?"

Marlow chuckles. "Not for much. She wasn't wanting money or anything like that. Well, not too much money because I'd made it clear that I didn't have all that much. She just wanted a little something, a little thing she thought I could easily get her."

Again, I knew where this was heading, but wanted the man to commit himself. "She wanted a job?"

The chuckle again, though a bit strained this time. "Not just any job. Something in City Hall, something important. Poor kid, she thought that was the golden ticket."

"She realize she probably made more doing hair, especially when you count in tips, than most city employees?"

Marlow slumped even further. If he got much more relaxed, he'd melt down into the floorboard. "I tried to explain it, but no matter what I said, she wouldn't see clearly. Said if I didn't get her some kind of decent gig, something important, she'd spill the beans."

"About you and her?"

Marlow turned to look out the window.

"How'd you leave it?" I prodded him.

"How do you think?" He continued staring at the parking lot outside, and I wondered what he saw there. "Told her I'd do what I could. Said to give me a few weeks to work something out so it'd look legitimate, then I bailed."

I drummed my fingers on the armrest and pondered things for

a bit. A glimmer of something came to me, and I took another few minutes to work it out in my head.

"This the first time she tried something like that? The first time she brought up going public on you?"

The mayor shook his head, then turned my way again. For a minute there, I saw in his eyes a sad, frightened little boy. "She'd been talking that way for a couple of months. I kept putting her off and putting her off, but she was getting so damned insistent. The last few weeks I began to worry she actually would try something."

"You tell anyone about it?"

Marlow shrugged and looked down at the floorboards. I wondered if it would help speed things along to haul him out of the car and slap him around. If not for the possible assault charge, I probably would've done it.

"Mr. Mayor?"

"A couple of people," he said, still downcast. It seemed like since I'd gotten in the car he'd spent the majority of time looking anywhere except at me.

"And you're afraid someone may have, what, taken it on themselves to solve the problem for you?"

He swiveled his head and locked gazes with me, for the first time really looking straight on. "That's exactly what I'm afraid of."

"You have any notion of who?" I asked.

He kept the straight on gaze for a moment, then turned away, more red creeping up his neck. "I've got my suspicions, sure. Nothing I want to share with anyone."

"How long you had these suspicions? Since her death?"

His head shook, but he still couldn't look at me. "Naw. When it first happened, like everyone else I figured the boyfriend. Even had someone keep an eye on the investigation, quietly, to keep me clued in."

"The cops eliminated Granger pretty quickly," I said.

He turned back to me, the look in his eyes reminding me of a lost puppy. "Uh huh. So then I assumed the same as most people. Some sort of random attacker that got carried away."

I took a breath, filling my lungs in order to calm myself. "Then I started snooping around."

He nodded, his eyes still looking lost, though with a tiny glint of anger back in them. "That's right. I get word of some low-rent private license snooping around the thing. By then, I'm confused as hell. Didn't know what to think."

I let out the breath, things beginning to clear up. "And then Matt Reynolds got killed."

Marlow nodded again. "The main cop investigating her murder, and he gets put down?"

"I'm guessing about then you began to get scared."

A flash of anger this time and a new edge in the voice. "Not scared, you no good snooper. I've never been scared of . . ." He wound down, and his head dipped, his chins touching his chest. "Yeah, you're right. Scared. Obviously, this was something bigger than I'm used to. And there I was right in the middle of it."

"Maybe not," I said. "Could have been wrong place, wrong time all around."

"Meaning what?"

"Meaning whoever it was may not have known you'd be around that night. They may not have intended for you to be involved at all."

He nodded, still facing me square on. "Either way, doesn't really feel like it matters now. I've had enough, Quinton. I'm willing to take my lumps for running around with younger women, but not for murder."

"You think they'll let it get that far?" I asked. "Why try to protect you just to hang you out to dry?"

"You don't get it, do you? I'm a commodity, mister. I can be bought and sold on a whim, and there's always more commodities waiting in the wings. So their plan to help me out backfired. No biggee. They'll just pluck the next sap in line and set him up for the big time."

"Leaving you to twist in the wind, whether you're indicted or not," I said.

"Now you're getting it."

"Then why are we sitting here, mayor? What do you want from me?"

"I want to hire you," Marlow said.

I blinked a couple of times. "Come again?

"Said I want to hire you. I think I've pretty much dodged this bullet, seeing as they've got no real evidence against me. But somewhere down the line something else is going to happen, and there's a good chance whoever did this is going to consider me a lost cause."

I wasn't so sure that Marlow was off the hook as far as the Mosby case. Like a lot of politicians, he worked only in terms of the immediate. If the cops had had him, then let him go, that must mean he was cleared.

While that's not how it usually worked out, I didn't see the point in correcting him at the moment. Whether he was still in the cops' crosshairs or not was his problem. But if someone else were involved in this whole mess, that was another issue.

"You want to smoke them out now? Get it all out and done with?"

Marlow nodded vigorously. "That's exactly what I want. What do you say?"

"My rates are rather high," I said. "For you, I'll run a special."

"Which is?"

I told him my special rates, which I made up on the spot and are basically triple my usual ones, and after a moment he nodded agreement. "I can do that. When do you start?"

"We have a deal?" I asked.

"I said yes. You have my word. When do you start?"

CHAPTER FORTY-SIX

I N ORDER FOR THINGS TO WORK OUT, I needed to take another run at Tyler Phelps. But trying to get to see him in his office again probably wasn't the best of approaches. I spent most of the evening trying to figure it out, while watching the local university's basketball team go through an absolute nail-biter of an almost-win and by around ten thought I had at least the makings of a plan in mind.

I grabbed my phone and began making calls. The first was to Talia Sanderson. I knew from seeing her the last several months that this was the night each month of the university's board meeting, and even if she didn't have to attend she usually made a point to. She'd explained it to me once.

"We've got the four different campuses, scattered around the state, and the board members are just as scattered. But one night a month they all come flocking into Providence to do their official duty. Since I live here anyway, it seems the least I can do is take a couple of hours out of a month to show up."

Must have been an early night for the ole' board because when I called her Talia answered right away.

"You're home early," I said.

"Pretty much a nothing night. About ten really minor items, each of which went through on a single vote."

"I'd assume summer meetings would be the important ones," I said. "Isn't that the perfect time to start plotting out exorbitant tuition increases, how to squeeze more work out of the non-tenured teachers, and all that kind of stuff?"

"I do believe, Mr. Quinton, that you hold a rather dim view of my profession."

"Only the people at the very top," I said. "Speaking of which, how are you getting along with Raymond Withers these days?"

"The chancellor of the university? Better than you."

"What makes you say that?" I asked.

"Well, last I remember he's never tried to throw me off the campus."

"He didn't try to throw me off," I explained. "Merely let it be known I wasn't welcome coming around."

Talia laughed, and I felt my night lightening with just the sound. "Sounds like throwing off to me. Why are you asking about Raymond?"

"I need some information," I said. "And since he's one of the movers and shakers in town, he may know what I need."

"So what you're saying is you want me to be a spy for you?" Her tone had gone from light to carefully controlled.

"Not really spy. More like ask him a couple of questions and relay the answers to me."

"If you two are such buddies, why not ask him yourself?"

"I would," I said, "but the last time I came around he tried to have me thrown off the campus."

Another laugh, slightly higher-pitched this time. "And if I do this favor for you, what's in it for me?"

"My undying gratitude?" I asked.

"Try again, buster. A girl can't live on gratitude."

"Then how's about dinner at the joint of your choice in Kansas City next weekend."

"Now you're talking. What is it you want me to check out with Withers?"

We talked a bit longer, me filling Talia in on the direction of her inquiries before hanging up for the night. I then glanced at the clock, saw it wasn't too late to bother someone, especially an intrepid local reporter, and placed another call to Angie Tickman.

She explained she was in the middle of rewriting a feature piece for next Sunday's edition. Even so, she took a few minutes to hear me out. After agreeing, with some mild arm-twisting, I hung up again and thought of who else to call.

I considered reaching out to Sean O'Flaherty, but decided owing more than one favor per year to the local mob boss wasn't that hot of a policy, so I made a quick mental list of four or five people I knew, mainly former clients, who were high enough up in either the social or political circles of Providence to possibly spread the word I wanted spread.

I managed to get hold of each one, explained the message I wanted relayed around town, and after the last call hung up for the night. Then a couple of hours of mindless gazing at an old black and white movie on TCM and into bed.

If I was lucky the whole Laura Mosby/Bob Marlow thing would be a wrap within the next twenty-four hours.

If the word I'd sent out managed to find the right set of ears.

I had no firm idea yet who those ears belonged to, though I figured I could manage an educated guess or two, but I hoped by some point tomorrow night I wouldn't have to guess at all.

CHAPTER FORTY-SEVEN

IT TURNED OUT NOT TO BE TALIA OR ANGIE. One of my former clients, a banker who'd hired me last year and for whom I'd managed to track down an employee who'd embezzled a couple of hundred thousand dollars from one of his branches, came through. He called around eight the next morning and gave me the info I'd needed.

He only requested I not reveal his name in any way. Made sense.

This former client was rich, respected and, at least locally, powerful, but not as powerful or rich as the man I was hunting.

Straight up at noon, I pulled my Cherokee into the parking lot of a private health club on Providence's far south side. Years ago, when I moved here at the end of my wrestling career, the south side was about ten square miles of scrubland and woods. Now, in a relatively short amount of time, it had been developed, partitioned, divided, and subdivided until it was the new money and power locus of Carson County.

The health club I'd pulled into was so exclusive it didn't even have a sign or the name on the front of the building, and I'd heard, though I didn't know this for sure, that the yearly membership ran into the low six figures, and that was just for the basic amenities.

The weather was typical summer hot, and we hadn't had rain for over a week, but the trees and lawn of this place were so bright green it almost pierced the eyes.

Even people who patronized places like this usually couldn't get away around the noon hour, so the secluded parking lot only held a dozen cars, of which my Cherokee clearly held the lowest Blue Book value.

The lobby looked more like the entryway for a telemarketing company than a gym or health club. Silver walls, slate gray floors and a white receptionist counter, all unrelieved by any plants or even a smidge of bright color. There was a pearl gray reception counter against the far wall and behind that a pair of pitch-black double doors.

Far as I could tell, the only piece of furniture in the place was the chair I assumed the young woman behind the counter sat on.

I guess people who can afford to work out in places like that didn't have to wait their turn for machines.

"Can I help you?" the receptionist asked. I could only see her from the neck up. She was a pretty brunette whose facial angles suggested she was in good trim.

"Tyler Phelps," I said. "I'd like to see him."

She gave me the once over, then looked at me a second time in a way suggesting she was about to call security. I grinned, hoping to defuse any suspicions.

"I'm a business partner of his," I said. As she looked even more doubtful than a moment before, I expanded the smile. "Was doing some roadwork earlier and didn't have time to change into my Gucci sweats," I explained.

Now she gave me a look she probably reserved for unwanted salesmen. "I think you need to leave, sir."

As she spoke, her left hand drifted off to the side, no doubt headed for a warning button or switch.

"Don't worry about it," I said. "I'll make sure you don't get in trouble for this."

I swept around the counter and headed for the double doors. The woman at the counter started to say something else, and in my peripheral vision I could see her jabbing at something under the counter, but I ignored all that.

The doors, lighter in weight than they appeared, swung open

at barely a touch, and I was in a large, open room with all sorts of workout equipment, mats, clothing racks and, along the far back wall, a row of semi-private saunas.

This time of day, a grand total of eight men were in the room, active at various weight stations, ellipticals, and machines.

No women around, I noticed.

So much for the progressive politics of our fair city.

Most of the men turned and glanced at me as I came in, probably wondering why I'd gotten confused as to where the delivery door was located. One or two were so focused on what they were doing to their bodies I probably could have exploded a bomb and they'd keep right on lifting, grunting, and perspiring.

Tyler Phelps was one of the ones who noticed me.

He lay half reclined on a weight bench, a pair of dumbbells in his hands, and taking a break doing some sort of press. Flanking each side of him were two large, tough-looking men in slacks and blazers, one wearing tan pants with a navy blazer and the other wearing the same colors but with the order switched.

As I headed his way, ignoring the other men, Phelps put down the weights and stared at me. With so few clients in the room at the time, my destination had to be pretty clear, but Phelps still gave me a puzzled look.

I didn't quite understand his confusion till I got within a yard of him, both of his goombahs tensing up at my approach.

Then Phelps snapped his fingers. "Quinlow, right?" he asked.

I sighed, realizing his confusion had come from the fact he didn't remember me.

"Close," I said. "Quinton. Sam Quinton."

A little light seemed to flare up in the eyes of Security Goon #1, he of the tan pants and blue blazer.

"Right," Phelps said. "Quinton. You're the guy who came to see me the other day."

"Without an appointment," I added, trying to be helpful.

Phelps shook his head and settled a little more firmly onto his half-reclined bench. "Without an appointment," he repeated. "I'd rather assumed our business was finished then. And now you're barging into a private facility. You don't seem to get messages very well, do you?"

"Mr. Phelps," Goon #1 said, "should we remove this gentleman?"

"Try it," I told the bodyguard, "and you'll end up in pieces."

"I don't think so, pal," the guard shot back. "I know you. Used to watch you try to wrestle back in St. Louis. Problem is," he pointed towards his counterpart, "Mr. Phelps here doesn't employ fake tough guys. He hires the real thing."

"You sure?" I asked. "I mean, how tough can you be in a blue blazer?"

The guy was obviously trained well because he didn't rise to my insult. Instead, he shook his head and looked to his boss for direction.

Phelps grabbed a towel from the rack behind him and wiped his face. "What do you want, Mr. Quinton? I assume it's something you think's important, so I'll give you two minutes before we find out who is and isn't tough around here."

"Fair enough," I said. "But I'll only need a minute at most."

Phelps nodded and leaned back on the bench. "Go on."

"His Honor, the mayor, has been in a lot of trouble recently."

"You barged in here to tell me what everyone in town already knows?" Phelps asked.

"But he may not be the only one in a jam."

"What do you mean? And what the hell's your interest in all this?"

"Simple," I said. "I'm a businessman. I'm looking to earn a little payday for myself."

"A payday for what? And your minute's about up."

"Then I'll make it fast," I said. "First, Laura Mosby was a smarter girl than most people gave her credit for."

"Meaning?"

"Meaning she had more going on than just His Honor."

"And second?"

"From what her friends tell me, she was good at keeping records. On her phone."

Phelps gave his two stiffs a sideways look. "You're even dumber than you look, Quinton. Don't you think the cops got her phone and computer?"

I grinned. "They got the phone they knew about. I've been snooping around this thing for a while now, and I keep hearing word about a second one she had. One a little more—private— shall we say, than her first one."

Phelps leaned forward now, his gaze intent on me. "What exactly do you want, Quinton?"

"I had a client when all this started, but then I got fired. The client said I wasn't producing results."

A bit of a fib but one I didn't think would get me in trouble down the line.

"So?" Phelps asked.

"So I've got a little deficit spending going on these days. How's about this? I grab her phone out of her house, and I get a nice bonus for turning it over to whoever wants it."

"What's to stop me from getting someone else to just waltz into her place and grab it up?"

"How about the fact that I have a pretty good guess where she kept it, so I could eliminate a lot of time searching. I've already been in her room once and seen the layout."

Phelps shook his head. "Maybe I don't care about any of this. As I told you before, sure, I'm one of the mayor's backers. And despite what you seem to imply, I think he's been damned good for this city."

"You think he'd make a damned good governor?" I asked.

"He would," Phelps said, leaning forward even more. "But so would several other people. And I didn't get to where I am by putting all of my paycheck on one horse, so to speak. What you seem to be hinting at is something I simply don't care all that much about. Not worth my trouble, if you will."

I shrugged. "That's a possibility. But maybe you know someone who would care. After all, can we all assume a murder charge is the worst thing Marlow has to face?"

"Give me a day," he said. "And I'll get back to you."

"Fair enough."

I gave the two stiffs in their pretty blazers a mock salute.

Then I turned and got out of there.

I could have pointed out to Phelps that he hadn't asked for my number, or any way to contact me, but assumed someone of his caliber wouldn't have any trouble tracking me down.

Then again, whether or not he did bother to reach out wasn't exactly the point of the little exercise.

CHAPTER FORTY-EIGHT

Later that afternoon, I was in my office going over some invoices when my desk phone buzzed.

"Sam," Keri Eckland said when I picked up, "there's a client here who wants to talk to you."

A small part of my gut clenched up. Old-time, chalk dust on the hands while pounding iron guy that I am, I never could quite get used to calling the people who used my gym "clients."

Once, I'd asked Lisa and Keri to come up with a different word so I wouldn't feel quite so out of date. They'd asked me for suggestions, I offered up "gym rats." At the looks the two gave me, I figured it better to drop the whole thing.

"A client?" I asked. "Is there a complaint or something?"

"I don't think so," Keri said. "Her name's Kylie Rogers, and she just asked if you were available."

With everything going on with the case, it had slipped my mind that, as she'd pointed out when I interviewed her last week, Laura Mosby's boss came by my gym now and then.

"Sure," I said, "send her in."

"Mr. Quinton," Kylie said. She wore a black skirt and jacket with a faint crimson pinstripe. Her eggshell blouse was open at the neck, and a small gold charm of some kind rested on a gold chain around her neck.

"Kylie," I said in response. "How you doing?"

She looked around the office a bit. "Can I sit down?"

"Sure."

She sat in one of the client chairs, back ramrod straight, and clasped her hands in her lap. She stayed that way for a few minutes before I decided to move things along.

"What can I do for you, Kylie?"

She hesitated a moment longer, looked around again. "Can we talk?"

"I think that's what we're doing," I said.

She giggled, blushed a bit, then looked down at the floor. "I mean really talk?"

"Of course," I said. "What's up? Lisa been restricting the number of towels guests can use again?"

The little joke got me another ten seconds or so of silence before she looked up at me. "I wasn't quite honest with you last week."

"Oh?"

"The cops were after Ryan from the beginning, right?"

"Ex-boyfriend of murdered woman? Sure, they were. But as far as they can tell he was clean of it."

"They think he was still into her?" Kylie asked.

I narrowed my eyes. "Why do you ask?"

She went silent again, her gaze focused somewhere beyond the wall behind me. "Ryan works in a warehouse, right? At least, he did when they were together."

"Still does. So what?"

Kylie fidgeted even more. "Laura had ambition," she finally said.

I had a hunch we were about to go over ground I already knew, but it seemed Kylie had to get something out of her system, so I decided to play along.

"Ambition? What kind?"

"Let's just say that spending her time with a laborer wasn't how she saw her life going."

"Such as?"

"Such as most of our clients are on the higher end of the socio-economic scale, right?"

"If you say so. Me, I usually only pay about fifteen dollars for a haircut, and that's counting the tip."

"Oh, believe me I do," Kylie said. "It's one of the downfalls of working in a place like *Extensions*. The tips are good, believe me. The money most of these women throw our way can really provide some comfort."

"Though not as much comfort as the clients themselves enjoy, right?"

Kylie nodded, and I thought I saw a faint glisten in her eyes. I wondered for a moment what it would be like to have a service job, especially in an establishment like hers. To spend your days and evenings waiting on people who, no matter how many hours or effort you put in, would always be above you on the monetary scale.

"It happens now and then," she said. "Someone new starts working, and before long they resent the lifestyle the clients have, at the same time they're hungering for it. When you see woman after woman pulling up in a Mercedes, or Porsche, or Tesla, and coming in wearing casual clothing that probably costs your monthly income, well, it can get a bit much sometimes."

I paused for a moment, giving the glisten a chance to disappear, before plunging back in. "Was Laura one of the ones it got to?"

A small sip of air escaped Kylie's lips. "Sort of. Although she was after slightly different stuff."

My pulse quickened a little. "Such as?"

"She didn't want money so much, though she wouldn't have turned it down. What she wanted was to be known, to be seen. To be a somebody of some sort."

"A somebody in Providence, Missouri?" I asked.

Kylie grinned, and a little spark flickered in her eyes. "Every place has to have someone everybody looks at."

"You didn't tell any of this to the cops back when?" I asked.

Kylie shook her head, ducking it down a bit. "At the time, I assumed like everyone it was Ryan. Didn't see the reason to trash Laura when she was dead."

"So why are you telling me now?"

Her head raised a bit, and the glisten had pretty much disappeared from her eyes. "'Cause I saw online the cops have arrested the mayor."

I thought fast. "Arrest" wasn't quite the right word, and I didn't know myself if word was out yet about Marlow's release, and while I didn't want to screw up any play Santiago's people had going, something told me Kylie here had something relevant on her mind.

"Not arrested," I said. "They took him in for questioning, but that's a long way from being charged. You know anything about it?"

"The mayor? Nope. Like I told you before, Laura didn't talk a lot about her personal life."

"Okay."

We sat for about thirty seconds this time.

"There's something more, though, isn't there Kylie," I said. "You're still not telling me everything, right?"

I expected her to deny it, but instead she nodded. "A few days before—before Laura didn't show up—a guy came around asking about her."

"Yeah?"

"Yeah," she growled. "Said he wanted to surprise his wife with a full makeover, hair and everything, and he'd heard Laura was good at her job and wanted to talk to her."

"Did he?"

Kylie shook her head. "Laura wasn't working that day, and I wasn't about to give out an employee's phone number to anyone, possible client or not. He gave me his number and asked me to have her call him. I took the number, but of course, she never got the message."

"Was this Mayor Marlow?" I asked.

"You know, up to this morning I didn't even know what the man looked like. But I looked him up online, and it wasn't him."

"I don't quite see the problem here. If you've got information, why not take it to the cops?"

"Are you serious? If this is something big enough to involve the mayor, you think I want to put myself out there like that?"

"But it's okay for me to?" I asked.

Her face scrunched a bit, and she began twisting her hands back and forth. "I didn't mean—I mean, this is what you do for a living, right?"

It occurred to me that setting myself up as a target wasn't exactly in my job description, then I realized in the last week or so I'd twice done exactly that.

"Kylie," I said, "this was months ago. How do you remember this guy coming by and all? You must meet dozens of people a day at your place."

"'Course I do. But trust me, everything about that week is burned into my memory."

"What'd the guy look like? You remember?"

She shrugged her shoulders. "Pretty much an average guy. Average height, weight. Nothing really stood out about him."

"Come on, help me out here. You work with people's appearance all the time. Anything about hair? Eye color? Anything like that?"

"What can I tell you, man? I'm thinking he was kind of brownish. And kind of out of shape."

"How do you mean?"

She shrugged. "Just that I looked at him and thought he should harden himself up a bit. But really, he was just, you know, a guy."

She wasn't even remotely describing the mayor, but I had an idea who she was talking about.

I pulled out my phone and scrolled around a bit before I found the picture I wanted. A couple of days before, I'd spent some time online and had downloaded a number of images. I then handed the phone over to Kylie.

A brief look, no more than half a second, before she nodded in the affirmative. "Yeah," she said, "that looks like him. Who is it?"

I didn't want to tell her, but I was pretty sure she'd just ID'd for me Laura Mosby's killer.

CHAPTER FORTY-NINE

WITH THE SUN JUST GOING DOWN, I parked about three blocks from Laura Mosby's house and walked the rest of the way. A glance around to make sure no one was out and about, and I slipped around back and let myself in.

The night was a typical Midwestern evening in June. Even so, before heading out I'd slipped on a light cotton jacket. As soon as I got inside and away from any possibly snoopy neighbors, I shucked the jacket, revealing the shoulder holster containing my gun.

I didn't turn on any lights, wanting the house to retain its deserted air. I figured it at fifty-fifty I'd have a visitor in the next few hours. More, I hoped it would be the person I expected.

I made a quick stop in the kitchen to drink down a glass of cold water before moving into Laura's bedroom. Grabbing the small white chair I'd noticed on my previous visit, I positioned myself along the wall next to the door and sat down to wait.

I crossed my arms and leaned my chair back against the wall. Before too long, the small amount of light that had found its way through the closed blinds of the windows petered out, and bit by bit darkness crept over the room.

I waited.

I kept as still as possible and focused on my breathing, trying to calm down. I consider myself a fairly tough guy, but no matter how tough you are, or think you are, if you're not careful sitting in the dark and waiting for a killer to show up can mess with the mind.

Through the slit of the window curtains I saw the streetlights come on, providing barely perceptible more illumination than before. I continued waiting, every now and then wondering if it was all for nothing.

Maybe the guy hadn't heard any of the whispers I'd sent around for him to pick up.

Maybe he'd heard them, but decided he was safe enough and why risk another visit to the crime scene.

Or maybe that slight creak was him stepping in the front door, though in almost the same instant I heard it I realized it was probably only the sound of the house settling.

At some point in the dark night, the overpowering urge came over me to pull out my phone and call Talia, listen to her voice for a while to help pass the time. A stupid idea, of course, because the whole point of this exercise was for Laura Mosby's killer to show up so I could get the drop on him.

I also considered, for about the fifth time in the last twenty-four hours, calling up Santiago and laying the whole thing out for him. After all, he and his people were paid to do this kind of thing; it was their job. And while I'd originally had a paying client, the lieutenant himself, I was unemployed as of a few days ago.

Another creak, a bit louder this time, and I wondered once again if my quarry had somehow snuck into the house without me hearing him. I held my breath and waited, holding myself so still my muscles actually hurt, but I couldn't detect any other noises.

I turned and looked at the bare bed frame, all that remained of where Laura Mosby had slept, dreamt, and died. For a moment, I tried to imagine what those last few minutes of her life had felt like, what she must have seen, heard and experienced.

I couldn't do it. Suffering a violent death is something that, quite obviously, I hadn't experienced yet, and I had no way to fit myself into her shell.

My thoughts then, almost without effort, turned to Bob Marlow, the now-disgraced mayor of Providence. I thought about how the man's entire life had crumbled around him in a matter of days, and wondered how much blame I should shoulder for that.

Even if, as I now believed, he was innocent, once his political opponents were done playing games with the events of the last several days, he'd be a dead man walking. And unless I was successful in my attempt, the taint of suspicion would follow him forever.

Hell, even if I did pull it off, the same would probably happen.

At first, I tried to cast myself as almost innocent. After all, I hadn't been the one to kill a girl, attempt to cover it up, then try throwing an innocent man to the wolves. I wasn't the one who gunned down Matt Reynolds in a city alleyway.

And while I wouldn't have gone so far as to call Marlow another victim in this mess, it seemed fairly obvious, at least to me, that he wasn't the murdering blackheart Santiago had suspected.

In fact, if all my suppositions were finally correct, if I was at last on the right track, Marlow was, if anything, almost a side issue.

I mentally crossed my fingers that I'd soon have it all in hand.

Another twenty minutes or so of waiting, though it was hard to tell time without seeing a clock or actually doing anything, and another faint sound came to my ears.

Not a creak of wood this time, instead the slight rubbing against frame as a somewhat-warped old door opened.

Uh huh.

Another few seconds, and straining my hearing I picked up a few faint brushing sounds, as of someone trying to walk quietly but managing only to scuffle along the floor.

As far as I figured, the intruder couldn't possibly suspect anyone else of being in the house. But most people, when engaged in some sort of sneaky activity, go out of their way to be silent even when not necessary.

The noises stopped in front of the bedroom doorway. I'd left the door open, of course, because why would a door in an abandoned house be closed? I wasn't sure why he stopped unless it was a sudden onset of nerves at the thought of entering.

Maybe a guilty conscience?

After a long moment I heard something so muted it could have only been the slightest of motion, maybe clothes rustling against each other, before there came a deep breath, and Stan Raimes, chief of staff to the mayor of Providence, walked into the room.

CHAPTER FIFTY

HE STOOD FOR A MOMENT just inside the bedroom doorway, keys dangling in his left hand.

His right held a handgun.

In the bedroom's gloom, I couldn't quite make out the model, but all things considered it really wouldn't have mattered.

What mattered was he had the gun; he was in the room with me; and even in the murk I could see his hand shaking.

The guy wasn't a pro, at least when it came to killing. In fact, as I'd already determined, he was pretty much as amateur as amateur could get.

Didn't make him any less dangerous, though.

He hadn't noticed me yet, and I kind of wondered why he didn't turn on the lights as soon as he entered the room. A moment or two later, as I stood there and watched him tremble all over, I got it.

An amateur, for sure. With Laura Mosby no doubt the first person he'd ever killed, and although as sleazy as they come, I imagined the thought of entering this room, where I was pretty sure a few months before he'd strangled the life out of a young woman who'd never done anything to him, proved rather overpowering.

After a few minutes his trembling eased, and from my position in the corner parallel to the doorway I could see his arm reaching out for the light switch.

"Don't do it, Raimes," I said.

Raimes froze, his arm half extended, and craned his neck in my direction.

"Who's there?" he said. "What do you want?"

I moved out into the one small patch of light in the room, provided by the half-opened drapes along the other wall.

Raimes blinked his eyes, trying to focus his vision.

I moved closer into the light, close enough he could see my own weapon covering him.

"Quinton."

"Right."

"You going to shoot me?" he asked. He was trying to keep his voice light, but the strain of holding his gun aloft was beginning to show. He was starting to tremble again.

"Not unless I have to. But you and I are going to have a talk."

"About what?" Raimes tried, and failed, for a sneer.

"What do you think about? Look where we are."

"If you're going to ask about the Mosby cunt, I've got better things to do."

He half-turned, as if to brazenly walk out the door.

I pulled back the hammer on my own gun, and he froze.

"No," I said, "you don't have anything better to do. Not for a long time."

He glanced back at me, his body even more arched and tense than before. With my weapon, I motioned him to sit on the edge of the bed frame.

He gave me a look.

"It's either that or the floor, mister."

Raimes nodded and sat down, though I noticed he didn't release his own weapon.

Not exactly a Mexican standoff, though close enough.

"So what do you want?" he asked. "Your cop buddies are already gunning for the mayor. What more do you want?"

"Stan," I said as I used my foot to hook a small stool closer so I could sit myself, "you and I both know he didn't do it."

Raimes tried for a smirk, again, and once again wasn't cool or tough enough to pull it off. "What makes you say that? He sure looks guilty as hell. All those years I worked for him, I didn't know he was a pervert."

I shook my head, wondering how much more I could take before I said the hell with it and blew him away. "He doesn't seem like a pervert to me. Just sounds like he has an abundant desire for the company of women. You could argue that he's a little old to be running around with girls in their twenties, but it's still nothing illegal. Right?"

Raimes's weak, watery eyes shifted. "If you say so," he muttered.

"Well," I said, "to each his own. But if you think he's a perv for lusting after younger women all the time, what the hell does that make you?"

Raimes flinched backwards. "What do you mean? I'm just . . ."

"You're just breaking into the house of a murder victim. Or maybe not so much breaking in, as you have her keys. Got to admit, I didn't expect that. Then again, with your job I'm guessing you know all kinds of tricks around City Hall, so it probably wasn't too difficult to filch them out of the evidence room. What'd you do? Bribe some poor clerk to get them?"

"Does it really matter?" Raimes asked.

"Not really," I said. "Which kind of leads to the question of why you're here? Afraid you left something behind last time you were here? Or do you just want to bask in the afterglow?"

"Doesn't matter why I'm here. What matters is I've got this gun focused on you."

"True," I said as I gave my own weapon a slight twirl. "But I've got mine trained on you, and I'm going to go out on a limb here and take the chance I'm more used to holding a weapon than you are. Tell me, Raimes, is yours starting to get a little heavy?"

"What if it is?" he snapped, and once more the bravado came off as forced.

"See," I said, "here's how I've got it figured. It's clear your boss had something going with Laura Mosby. Even putting aside the fact that he admitted it to me, the cops found this room lousy with his DNA. On top of that, at least one of his political opponents had cottoned to it as well. But I don't think he killed her."

"Oh?" The single word, but I noticed the barrel of his weapon starting to dip a bit.

"I think he was with her the night she died, as he claims, and probably stayed as long as he could before her nagging got to him and he had to get home to the little wife. That's his story, and to me it makes sense. After all, got to maintain that wholesome public image, especially if he's going to run for governor."

"If he managed to get that far," Raimes grumbled, the barrel dropping lower. "If he could only have stopped dipping his wick in every slut that went by, he would have had a chance. But he couldn't help himself."

"Right," I said, "that's the story going around, isn't it? There's a lot of possible theories as to what happened next. I'm sure the cops are making a list. Want to hear them?"

"I don't give a damn about . . ."

"One notion has it he started strangling her in kinky play, and it got out of hand."

Raimes said nothing, but only glared at me.

"Another theory is that she was threatening him in some way, and he killed her to shut her up. Both ideas, by the way, he completely denies."

Raimes continued his glare. Had I not been an ex-jock and world-class tough guy, I may have worried a little. But I could also see his arm trembling with the strain of holding up his weapon.

"But I've got another idea," I said.

Had Raimes actually been a professional at this sort of thing, he would have continued keeping quiet. But being the amateur he was, he couldn't resist. "Which is?"

"I think Marlow came over here that night, had his little romp with Miss Mosby, then went home. Just like he says happened. And I think some time after, you showed up."

Raimes's face blanched, and a tic developed under his left eye. "I don't know what the hell you're talking about."

Grinning, I shook my head and noticed his arm wobble even

more. "I think you do. It could have been for one of two things, and I'm not quite sure which."

"What do you mean? What things?"

"Sorry," I said. "I meant motivation. First scenario you, being the loyal servant to the big man that you are, get concerned the mayor's little side actions will become public knowledge and mess up his shot at the governorship. Considering that Lou Sanders out of Rolla has an operative dogging the mayor's trail, that's a pretty safe assumption."

Raimes blanched at my mention of Sanders's name.

"But there's a couple of other possibilities," I said.

"Like what?"

I did a half shrug, not wanting to disrupt our standoff with the guns. "According to Marlow and some other information I dug up, Laura was trying to blackmail him. You got word of it. Either he told you directly, or you figured it out some other way. Marlow says that all she wanted was a city job so she could get out of the hair racket. Then again, he is a politician, which means I have to be skeptical of everything he says. Could be Laura wanted him to divorce his wife and move her up in society. Maybe she saw herself someday hosting parties at the governor's mansion. Who the hell knows?"

"In other words you're speculating." There was a little gasp at the end of his sentence, and I figured the gun was getting really heavy.

"Of course, I'm speculating. Hell, I wasn't there, and the only person I've spoken to who was there is the mayor himself. And you and I both know how honest and forthright he is. So how the hell would I know for sure? But given any one of the possibilities I mentioned, I can see His Honor may have complained to you a little, which could have led you to decide to help your boss out."

"By killing the bitch? That's what you think?"

I did another partial shrug. My grip was starting to cramp a little, making me guess Raimes's hand and arm were really feeling it. "Not necessarily. Maybe you came out here to talk to her, try to reason with her, and it went bad. You know, she laughed in your face or something, and you struck out."

"I'm not saying a thing to this nonsense, Quinton."

I gave him a smile and tried to put a little menace into it. "You don't really have to, you know. Unlike all the stuff you see on TV, the prosecutors don't really need to have a motive to put someone's ass away. It helps of course, but they're much more interested in proving the who than the why."

He peered at me and leaned over, his face beginning to redden. "As long as you're talking, and I'm not about to say anything, what's your other scenario?"

"Aw," I said, "that one's a whole lot simpler. You saw Laura cavorting with the big guy and decided you wanted some of that too. After all, why should a slimeball like Marlow get all the goodies for himself? After he left that night, you came over to put the moves on her, she gave you a 'Get the hell out of here creep' speech, and you lost it."

His gun barrel had dropped so far it was now pointed somewhere around my kneecaps.

Good, but not good enough.

"Interesting ideas," Raimes said, "but they don't really matter all that much, do they?"

"Nope. Like I said, the cops are going to be far more interested in the who than the why. And now that we've got that main little question all sewed up . . ."

"What makes you think it's sewed?" Raimes had shifted his weapon up a bit, his eyes taking on a new gleam.

"Mainly," I said, "because you're not going to kill me, Stan."

"And what makes you think so?"

I shook my head and slouched a bit, making myself a little less of an immediate threat. "Couple of things. One, you're not a stone-cold killer."

Now it was Raimes's turn to shake his head. "I thought you said I killed the Mosby girl."

"Sure." I nodded in agreement. "In a rage, for some reason or other. On the spur of the moment, maybe. But not like this. Not with her sitting across from you, talking to you like I am. Having the time to prepare is a whole 'nother level of killing."

"I killed a man the other day."

The one loose end in this entire affair had just been tucked into place. I tried to keep my feeling of sudden rage off my face.

"Matt Reynolds?" I asked.

"That's right. What do you say about that?"

"You did," I said as my arm began to tingle a little. "And it probably went something like this. Detective Reynolds wanted to question you. You probably suggested a hidden meeting place by saying you wanted to come clean. Maybe something along the lines of you had the lowdown on Marlow and wanted to do right but were scared the mayor would find out and come after you. Something like that to get him alone in an alley with you?"

"That's what I told him, sure. Truth, though, what I really wanted was to get him to lay off. To leave the mayor alone. He's worked for the city long enough that I thought I could talk to him, but he wouldn't even listen. All he wanted to know was anything about the mayor. He wouldn't listen to reason. Then I said something stupid."

I could imagine a whole lot of dumb things he could have possibly said. "Which was?"

Raimes shook a bit more than before, and his voice by now had developed a distinct quaver. "I asked him where his partner was. I thought maybe she would listen to reason."

I shook my head. "Foolish. My guess is Reynolds was doing everything possible to protect Krenshaw from any political fallout. After all, he was the veteran in the department, not her. You mentioning her probably set him off somewhat."

"It did. Next thing I knew he was looming over me, trying to impose like you see cops do on TV. I panicked."

I could see it clearly in my head. Matt Reynolds talking with this nebishy little guy in an alley alone. Knowing him from around City Hall and having no way of knowing Raimes had already killed. Matt not expecting himself to be in any sort of danger.

And Raimes getting the drop on a guy only trying to wrap a case and protect his partner.

"Like I said, you're a newbie at this. And there's one thing I can see for sure you haven't learned yet."

"Which is?"

Now I smiled at him, reaching all the way back to my wrestling days and giving him the old Blond Bomber smile full force. "Well," I said, "if you really intended to shoot me, wouldn't you have made sure you had a clip in the gun?"

Raimes's face sagged, then tightened, and he glanced down at his weapon.

In the flash of a second when he looked down, I lunged.

CHAPTER FIFTY-ONE

RAIMES WAS FASTER THAN I'D EXPECTED. As he flicked his gaze down to his gun, I sprang out of my chair and covered the four feet between us. I twisted my own weapon in such a way as to smash the butt across his face and, hopefully, put a quick end to this.

But the dude recovered just as I reached him and, through either sheer dumb luck or extreme cunning, made a move I didn't expect.

He jabbed his weapon, still held straight in front of him, barrel first into my abdomen.

A blinding stab of pain hit me, centered on only one small area in my stomach but nearly taking the breath away, and I stumbled to my knees, dropping my gun as I did so. He lifted his hand up, no doubt intending to bring the gun's butt down on the top of my head, but I managed to swerve a few inches to the side and roll away.

This put the two of us approximately the same distance apart as before, but with one crucial difference. Raimes still had ahold of his weapon, while mine was a couple of feet away from me.

A cool professional would have quickly sighted down and blown me away.

Someone a little more psychopathic would have taken the time to titter and jeer before doing me in.

Raimes, still an apprentice killer, froze, gawked at me kneeling before him, the trembling returning as he worked up the nerve to shoot me down.

Of course, I didn't give him the time.

Straight from the floor, I tackled him around the knees and hurled him back onto the metal bed frame. The frame wasn't thick enough to crack his head or anything, but the shock of my two hundred plus pounds plowing onto his torso drove the breath out of him, and a quick chop of my hand caused his gun to drop to the floor alongside mine.

In the background, I heard a door slam open. I ignored it as I reared up and brought my right hand down, palm flat, onto Raimes's chest. It's a move you see wrestlers do a lot, and even when we pull our punches it can produce a stinging impact on an opponent's body.

I didn't pull my punch, not in the least. Raimes gurgled a little, and his eyes rolled up in his head.

When I stood up, he flopped over on the floor, out of it for the moment. I took a step back, noticing I was breathing a little hard. Wasn't sure if it was from the exertion or the excitement, and at the moment it didn't matter.

To my side, the bedroom doorway darkened a bit, and I looked over to see Abbie Krenshaw standing there, her own pistol out and covering Raimes, who lay on his side gasping for air and retching a little.

"What kept you?" I asked.

Krenshaw grimaced and reached into her jacket pocket to pull out her handcuffs. "At the last minute, the review board on Matt's homicide called me in for some followup. Didn't want to look anxious to leave, in case they thought I had something to hide."

She snapped the cuffs on Raimes, then turned him over on his side. He was still struggling a little to get his breath back.

"I'll be damned," she said. "So the mayor wasn't guilty after all."

I grinned at her. "At least not for this. I'm sure if you feel like it you can keep digging and find some skeletons in his closet somewhere."

Krenshaw shook her head. "No thanks. One political bust a decade is enough for me."

"In that case, Detective, why don't you take your suspect away and put him where he belongs."

Yanking Raimes up by his shoulder, she did just that.

CHAPTER FIFTY-TWO

Santiago came by my place three days after Stan Raimes's arrest.

"Wanted to thank you personally for what you did," he said, looking uncomfortable standing in my doorway.

To preserve what little subtlety was left, we'd agreed to meet up at my apartment instead of the gym.

I ushered him inside, and after a moment he entered. Hard to believe a man wearing probably two thousand dollars-worth of gray pinstriped suit, hand-tailored French cuff shirt, and lambskin tasseled loafers could look uncomfortable, but there you go.

Maybe he should try jeans and a tee-shirt sometime.

"You expecting someone?" he asked as I shut the door behind us.

I glanced down at the apron tied around my waist. "What would you say if I said I was just working on my culinary skills?"

"I'd say your concept of culinary is probably frozen pizza with Cheez Whiz melted on top."

I made a face and headed back to the kitchen. Talia was going to be over as soon as she managed to pull herself away from work, and I was keeping an eye on the cacciatore.

Santiago followed me until he leaned against the kitchen door-frame. "Word is the mayor's going to make an announcement tonight. He won't be running for governor next fall."

"Be better if he resigned," I said as I fussed over the chicken.

"Maybe," Santiago's tone pretty much shrieked that he agreed with me, "but I learned long ago you take what you can get and call it good. No matter how much it digs at you."

I glanced up from the stove and looked his way. "Chicago?" I asked.

Santiago nodded, his eyes looking somewhere other than at me.

"Someday," I said, "you'll have to tell me how you ended up here in Providence."

The eyes snapped back to the here and now, fully focused. "Not bloody likely, Quinton. Anyway, I basically stopped by to thank you for what you did."

"Thanks are fine," I said, "but a check would be better."

Santiago cracked a grin. "Voucher was submitted this morning."

"Great," I said, keeping half an eye on the pans on the stove, "means I should get paid somewhere around the time the university holds graduation next May."

Santiago's grin widened. "Welcome to working for the public purse."

"No thanks," I said as I grabbed a bottle of wine off the counter and began working the cork. "Think I'll stay private."

"Your choice."

"What about Raimes?" I asked.

"DA plans to have an indictment drawn up within a day or so."

"So that's it," I said.

"Looks like it. Raimes is going to go away, and the mayor gets to eventually slink off into the sunset. Taken altogether, I'd say it's a good deal."

I leaned against the counter and crossed my arms. "It going to come out what a scuz His Honor is?"

"Don't think that's avoidable, especially once Raimes's trial starts. Probably why Marlow's decided not to run again. My guess would be, as soon as his term here's up, he'll take off for somewhere else."

It was less than avoidable, especially considering how much inside scoop I'd given Angie Tickman. Nothing that didn't come out from other sources, but enough of a head start that she'd been leading the pack for the last few days.

"Where the hell you been, Lieutenant? He'll be gone for a few years, maybe a year and a half, then come back playing the aggrieved victim and ride it all the way."

"Maybe so," Santiago said, "but I'll take the temporary victory right now and call it a day."

I started to reply, but a knock came at the door.

"Your dinner companion?" Santiago asked.

"One can hope," I said. "No offense, Lieutenant, but three's a crowd and all that."

The cop quirked another grin my way. "I'll let her in while I'm leaving."

"The hell you will," I said. "My place, my girl, and I open the door for her."

Two seconds later, I'd done just that, and Talia stood in the doorway, a light cotton jacket slung across her arm. She looked at Santiago.

"Dinner for three?"

"The hell," I said. "The good lieutenant was just leaving. Weren't you?"

"Absolutely," Santiago said. "Would it tarnish your image if I said good job one more time?"

"Don't you dare," I said, "or the doctor here will think I've softened up in my old age."

Santiago nodded to me, smiled at Talia, and left. I shut the door behind him and turned my full attention to my newest guest.

"He here to try to arrest you?" Talia asked.

I smirked and shook my head. "Wanted to thank me for a job well done."

She frowned for a moment, then the lines in her face smoothed out. "Wait a minute, buster. You telling me this big case of yours, the one you had to keep so hush hush about, you were working for the cops?"

"I was working for *a* cop, yeah."

"Well if the job's done, can you tell me about it now?"

"Tell you. Hell, girl, you've been hearing about it on the media for the last few days."

"Huh?"

Grinning, I grabbed her around the waist and began shepherding her to the dining room. "I'll make it all clear," I said, "but only after we eat. I don't want anything to spoil your concentration on the feast I've spent all day preparing for you."

She giggled, and those little laugh lines around her eyes crinkled up in that way that drove me crazy. "I'll hold you to it," she said.

"Hold me to what? That I've got a great meal ahead for you?"

"Hell, no, Quinton. That you'll tell me the story. For all I know, this feast of yours is just a warmed-up can of SpaghettiOs."

"Then you're about to be surprised on two fronts," I said as I held out a chair for her to sit.

And, truth be told, it turned out Talia had a few surprises for me that night as well.

A LIFELONG MIDWESTENER, KEVIN R. DOYLE TEACHES English at a small, rural high school in Missouri. He holds a bachelor's degree in English and a master's in communications, both from Wichita State University. While he spent several decades writing short stories, mainly in the horror field, in the last decade he's moved into longer works in the genres of crime, horror and rock fiction.

His first published "book" was actually a short novelette, *One Helluva Gig*, recently re-released by The Wild Rose Press. His first full-length book, a crime novel titled *The Group*, was followed by two sequels, *When You Have to Go There* and *And the Devil Walks Away*, all currently released by The Wild Rose Press.

Besides straight crime thrillers, he's also written four novels in the Sam Quinton private eye series, beginning with *Squatter's Rights*, nominated for a Shamus award for Best First Private Eye Novel of 2021.

In the horror field, in 2015 Night to Dawn Magazine and Books released his novel, *The Litter* and in 2022 will release a new mystery novel, *The Anchor*.